BLAC

OF   RS

BLACK AMAZON OF MARS

And Other Tales from the Pulps

LEIGH BRACKETT

BLACK AMAZON OF MARS AND OTHER TALES FROM THE PULPS

"Black Amazon of Mars" was originally published in *Planet Stories*, March 1951. "A World is Born" was originally published in *Comet Stories*, July 1941. "Child of the Sun" was originally published in *Planet Stories*, Spring 1942.

Published in 2010 by Wildside Press, LLC.
For more information, see
www.wildsidebooks.com

CONTENTS

BLACK AMAZON
OF MARS

I

Through all the long cold hours of the Norland night the Martian had not moved nor spoken. At dusk of the day before Eric John Stark had brought him into the ruined tower and laid him down, wrapped in blankets, on the snow. He had built a fire of dead brush, and since then the two men had waited, alone in the vast wasteland that girdles the polar cap of Mars.

Now, just before dawn, Camar the Martian spoke.

"Stark."

"Yes?"

"I am dying."

"Yes."

"I will not reach Kushat."

"No."

Camar nodded. He was silent again.

The wind howled down from the northern ice, and the broken walls rose up against it, brooding, gigantic, roofless now but so huge and sprawling that they seemed less like walls than cliffs of ebon stone. Stark would not have gone near them but for Camar. They were wrong, somehow, with a taint of forgotten evil still about them.

The big Earthman glanced at Camar, and his face was sad. "A man likes to die in his own place," he said abruptly. "I am sorry."

"The Lord of Silence is a great personage," Camar answered. "He does not mind the meeting place. No. It was not for that I came back into the Norlands."

He was shaken by an agony that was not of the body. "And I shall not reach Kushat!"

Stark spoke quietly, using the courtly High Martian almost as fluently as Camar.

"I have known that there was a burden heavier than death upon my brother's soul."

He leaned over, placing one large hand on the Martian's shoulder. "My brother has given his life for mine. Therefore, I will take his burden upon myself, if I can."

He did not want Camar's burden, whatever it might be. But the

Martian had fought beside him through a long guerilla campaign among the harried tribes of the nearer moon. He was a good man of his hands, and in the end had taken the bullet that was meant for Stark, knowing quite well what he was doing. They were friends.

That was why Stark had brought Camar into the bleak north country, trying to reach the city of his birth. The Martian was driven by some secret demon. He was afraid to die before he reached Kushat.

And now he had no choice.

"I have sinned, Stark. I have stolen a holy thing. You're an outlander, you would not know of Ban Cruach, and the talisman that he left when he went away forever beyond the Gates of Death."

Camar flung aside the blankets and sat up, his voice gaining a febrile strength.

"I was born and bred in the Thieves' Quarter under the Wall. I was proud of my skill. And the talisman was a challenge. It was a treasured thing—so treasured that hardly a man has touched it since the days of Ban Cruach who made it. And that was in the days when men still had the lustre on them, before they forgot that they were gods.

"'Guard well the Gates of Death,' he said, 'that is the city's trust. And keep the talisman always, for the day may come when you will need its strength. Who holds Kushat holds Mars—and the talisman will keep the city safe.'

"I was a thief, and proud. And I stole the talisman."

His hands went to his girdle, a belt of worn leather with a boss of battered steel. But his fingers were already numb.

"Take it, Stark. Open the boss—there, on the side, where the beast's head is carved. . . ."

Stark took the belt from Camar and found the hidden spring. The rounded top of the boss came free. Inside it was something wrapped in a scrap of silk.

"I had to leave Kushat," Camar whispered. "I could never go back. But it was enough—to have taken that."

He watched, shaken between awe and pride and remorse, as Stark unwrapped the bit of silk.

Stark had discounted most of Camar's talk as superstition, but even so he had expected something more spectacular than the object he held in his palm.

It was a lens, some four inches across—man-made, and made with great skill, but still only a bit of crystal. Turning it about, Stark saw that it was not a simple lens, but an intricate interlocking of many facets. Incredibly complicated, hypnotic if one looked at it too long.

"What is its use?" he asked of Camar.

"We are as children. We have forgotten. But there is a legend, a belief—that Ban Cruach himself made the talisman as a sign that he would not forget us, and would come back when Kushat is threatened. Back through the Gates of Death, to teach us again the power that was his!"

"I do not understand," said Stark. "What are the Gates of Death?"

Camar answered, "It is a pass that opens into the black mountains beyond Kushat. The city stands guard before it—why, no man remembers, except that it is a great trust."

His gaze feasted on the talisman.

Stark said, "You wish me to take this to Kushat?"

"Yes. Yes! And yet. . . ." Camar looked at Stark, his eyes filling suddenly with tears. "No. The North is not used to strangers. With me, you might have been safe. But alone. . . . No, Stark. You have risked too much already. Go back, out of the Norlands, while you can."

He lay back on the blankets. Stark saw that a bluish pallor had come into the hollows of his cheeks.

"Camar," he said. And again, "Camar!"

"Yes?"

"Go in peace, Camar. I will take the talisman to Kushat."

The Martian sighed, and smiled, and Stark was glad that he had made the promise.

"The riders of Mekh are wolves," said Camar suddenly. "They hunt these gorges. Look out for them."

"I will."

Stark's knowledge of the geography of this part of Mars was vague indeed, but he knew that the mountain valleys of Mekh lay ahead and to the north, between him and Kushat. Camar had told him of these upland warriors. He was willing to heed the warning.

Camar had done with talking. Stark knew that he had not long to wait. The wind spoke with the voice of a great organ. The moons had set and it was very dark outside the tower, except for the white glimmering of the snow. Stark looked up at the brooding walls, and shivered. There was a smell of death already in the air.

To keep from thinking, he bent closer to the fire, studying the lens. There were scratches on the bezel, as though it had been held sometime in a clamp, or setting, like a jewel. An ornament, probably, worn as a badge of rank. Strange ornament for a barbarian king, in the dawn of Mars. The firelight made tiny dancing sparks in the endless inner facets. Quite suddenly, he had a curious feeling that the thing was alive.

A pang of primitive and unreasoning fear shot through him, and he fought it down. His vision was beginning to blur, and he shut his eyes, and in the darkness it seemed to him that he could see and hear. . . .

He started up, shaken now with an eerie terror, and raised his hand to hurl the talisman away. But the part of him that had learned with much pain and effort to be civilized made him stop, and think.

He sat down again. An instrument of hypnosis? Possibly. And yet that fleeting touch of sight and sound had not been his own, out of his own memories.

He was tempted now, fascinated, like a child that plays with fire. The talisman had been worn somehow. Where? On the breast? On the brow?

He tried the first, with no result. Then he touched the flat surface of the lens to his forehead.

The great tower of stone rose up monstrous to the sky. It was whole, and there were pallid lights within that stirred and flickered, and it was crowned with a shimmering darkness.

He lay outside the tower, on his belly, and he was filled with fear and a great anger, and a loathing such as turns the bones to water. There was no snow. There was ice everywhere, rising to half the tower's height, sheathing the ground.

Ice. Cold and clear and beautiful—and deadly.

He moved. He glided snakelike, with infinite caution, over the smooth surface. The tower was gone, and far below him was a city. He saw the temples and the palaces, the glittering lovely city beneath him in the ice, blurred and fairylike and strange, a dream half glimpsed through crystal.

He saw the Ones that lived there, moving slowly through the streets. He could not see them clearly, only the vague shining of their bodies, and he was glad.

He hated them, with a hatred that conquered even his fear, which was great indeed.

He was not Eric John Stark. He was Ban Cruach.

The tower and the city vanished, swept away on a reeling tide.

He stood beneath a scarp of black rock, notched with a single pass. The cliffs hung over him, leaning out their vast bulk as though to crush him, and the narrow mouth of the pass was full of evil laughter where the wind went by.

He began to walk forward, into the pass. He was quite alone.

The light was dim and strange at the bottom of that cleft. Little veils of mist crept and clung between the ice and the rock, thickened, became more dense as he went farther and farther into the pass. He could not see, and the wind spoke with many tongues, piping in the crevices of the cliffs.

All at once there was a shadow in the mist before him, a dim gigantic shape that moved toward him, and he knew that he looked at death. He cried out. . . .

It was Stark who yelled in blind atavistic fear, and the echo of his own cry brought him up standing, shaking in every limb. He had dropped the talisman. It lay gleaming in the snow at his feet, and the alien memories were gone—and Camar was dead.

After a time he crouched down, breathing harshly. He did not want to touch the lens again. The part of him that had learned to fear strange gods and evil spirits with every step he took, the primitive aboriginal that lay so close under the surface of his mind, warned him to leave it, to run away, to desert this place of death and ruined stone.

He forced himself to take it up. He did not look at it. He wrapped it in the bit of silk and replaced it inside the iron boss, and clasped the belt around his waist. Then he found the small flask that lay with his gear beside the fire and took a long pull, and tried to think rationally of the thing that had happened.

Memories. Not his own, but the memories of Ban Cruach, a million years ago in the morning of a world. Memories of hate, a secret war against unhuman beings that dwelt in crystal cities cut in the living ice, and used these ruined towers for some dark purpose of their own.

Was that the meaning of the talisman, the power that lay within it? Had Ban Cruach, by some elder and forgotten science, imprisoned the echoes of his own mind in the crystal?

Why? Perhaps as a warning, as a reminder of ageless, alien danger beyond the Gates of Death?

Suddenly one of the beasts tethered outside the ruined tower started up from its sleep with a hissing snarl.

Instantly Stark became motionless.

They came silently on their padded feet, the rangy mountain brutes moving daintily through the sprawling ruin. Their riders too were silent—tall men with fierce eyes and russet hair, wearing leather coats and carrying each a long, straight spear.

There were a score of them around the tower in the windy gloom. Stark did not bother to draw his gun. He had learned very young the difference between courage and idiocy.

He walked out toward them, slowly lest one of them be startled into spearing him, yet not slowly enough to denote fear. And he held up his right hand and gave them greeting.

They did not answer him. They sat their restive mounts and stared at him, and Stark knew that Camar had spoken the truth. These were the riders of Mekh, and they were wolves.

II

Stark waited, until they should tire of their own silence.

Finally one demanded, "Of what country are you?"

He answered, "I am called N'Chaka, the Man-Without-a-Tribe."

It was the name they had given him, the half-human aboriginals who had raised him in the blaze and thunder and bitter frosts of Mercury.

"A stranger," said the leader, and smiled. He pointed at the dead Camar and asked, "Did you slay him?"

"He was my friend," said Stark, "I was bringing him home to die."

Two riders dismounted to inspect the body. One called up to the leader, "He was from Kushat, if I know the breed, Thord! And he has not been robbed." He proceeded to take care of that detail himself.

"A stranger," repeated the leader, Thord. "Bound for Kushat, with a man of Kushat. Well. I think you will come with us, stranger."

Stark shrugged. And with the long spears pricking him, he did not resist when the tall Thord plundered him of all he owned except his clothes—and Camar's belt, which was not worth the stealing. His gun Thord flung contemptuously away.

One of the men brought Stark's beast and Camar's from where they were tethered, and the Earthman mounted—as usual, over the violent protest of the creature, which did not like the smell of him. They moved out from under the shelter of the walls, into the full fury of the wind.

For the rest of that night, and through the next day and the night that followed it they rode eastward, stopping only to rest the beasts and chew on their rations of jerked meat.

To Stark, riding a prisoner, it came with full force that this was the North country, half a world away from the Mars of spaceships and commerce and visitors from other planets. The future had never touched these wild mountains and barren plains. The past held pride enough.

To the north, the horizon showed a strange and ghostly glimmer where the barrier wall of the polar pack reared up, gigantic against the sky. The wind blew, down from the ice, through the mountain gorges, across the plains, never ceasing. And here and there the cryptic towers rose, broken monoliths of stone. Stark remembered the vision of the talisman, the huge structure crowned with eerie darkness. He looked upon the ruins with loathing and curiosity. The men of Mekh could tell him nothing.

Thord did not tell Stark where they were taking him, and Stark did not ask. It would have been an admission of fear.

In mid-afternoon of the second day they came to a lip of rock where the snow was swept clean, and below it was a sheer drop into a narrow valley. Looking down, Stark saw that on the floor of the valley, up and down as far as he could see, were men and beasts and shelters of hide and brush, and fires burning. By the hundreds, by the several thousand, they camped under the cliffs, and their voices rose up on the thin air in a vast deep murmur that was deafening after the silence of the plains.

A war party, gathered now, before the thaw. Stark smiled. He became curious to meet the leader of this army.

They found their way single file along a winding track that dropped down the cliff face. The wind stopped abruptly, cut off by the valley walls. They came in among the shelters of the camp.

Here the snow was churned and soiled and melted to slush by the fires. There were no women in the camp, no sign of the usual cheerful rabble that follows a barbarian army. There were only men—hillmen and warriors all, tough-handed killers with no thought but battle.

They came out of their holes to shout at Thord and his men, and stare at the stranger. Thord was flushed and jovial with importance.

"I have no time for you," he shouted back. "I go to speak with the Lord Ciaran."

Stark rode impassively, a dark giant with a face of stone. From time to time he made his beast curvet, and laughed at himself inwardly for doing it.

They came at length to a shelter larger than the others, but built exactly the same and no more comfortable. A spear was thrust into the snow beside the entrance, and from it hung a black pennant with a single bar of silver across it, like lightning in a night sky. Beside it was a shield with the same device. There were no guards.

Thord dismounted, bidding Stark to do the same. He hammered on the shield with the hilt of his sword, announcing himself.

"Lord Ciaran! It is Thord—with a captive."

A voice, toneless and strangely muffled, spoke from within.

"Enter, Thord."

Thord pushed aside the hide curtain and went in, with Stark at his heels.

The dim daylight did not penetrate the interior. Cressets burned, giving off a flickering brilliance and a smell of strong oil. The floor of packed snow was carpeted with furs, much worn. Otherwise there was no adornment, and no furniture but a chair and a table, both dark with age and use, and a pallet of skins in one shadowy corner with what seemed to be a heap of rags upon it.

In the chair sat a man.

He seemed very tall, in the shaking light of the cressets. From neck to thigh his lean body was cased in black link mail, and under that a tunic of leather, dyed black. Across his knees he held a sable axe, a great thing made for the shearing of skulls, and his hands lay upon it gently, as though it were a toy he loved.

His head and face were covered by a thing that Stark had seen before only in very old paintings—the ancient war-mask of the inland Kings of Mars. Wrought of black and gleaming steel, it presented an unhuman visage of slitted eyeholes and a barred slot for breathing. Behind, it sprang out in a thin, soaring sweep, like a dark wing edge-on in flight.

The intent, expressionless scrutiny of that mask was bent, not upon Thord, but upon Eric John Stark.

The hollow voice spoke again, from behind the mask. "Well?"

"We were hunting in the gorges to the south," said Thord. "We saw a fire. . . ." He told the story, of how they had found the stranger and the body of the man from Kushat.

"Kushat!" said the Lord Ciaran softly. "Ah! And why, stranger, were you going to Kushat?"

"My name is Stark. Eric John Stark, Earthman, out of Mercury." He was tired of being called stranger. Quite suddenly, he was tired of the whole business.

"Why should I not go to Kushat? Is it against some law, that a man may not go there in peace without being hounded all over the Norlands? And why do the men of Mekh make it their business? They have nothing to do with the city."

Thord held his breath, watching with delighted anticipation.

The hands of the man in armor caressed the axe. They were slender hands, smooth and sinewy—small hands, it seemed, for such a weapon.

"We make what we will our business, Eric John Stark." He spoke with a peculiar gentleness. "I have asked you. Why were you going to Kushat?"

"Because," Stark answered with equal restraint, "my comrade wanted to go home to die."

"It seems a long, hard journey, just for dying." The black helm bent forward, in an attitude of thought. "Only the condemned or banished leave their cities, or their clans. Why did your comrade flee Kushat?"

A voice spoke suddenly from out of the heap of rags that lay on the pallet in the shadows of the corner. A man's voice, deep and husky, with the harsh quaver of age or madness in it.

"Three men beside myself have fled Kushat, over the years that matter. One died in the spring floods. One was caught in the moving ice of winter. One lived. A thief named Camar, who stole a certain talisman."

Stark said, "My comrade was called Greshi." The leather belt weighed heavy about him, and the iron boss seemed hot against his belly. He was beginning, now, to be afraid.

The Lord Ciaran spoke, ignoring Stark. "It was the sacred talisman of Kushat. Without it, the city is like a man without a soul."

As the Veil of Tanit was to Carthage, Stark thought, and reflected on the fate of that city after the Veil was stolen.

"The nobles were afraid of their own people," the man in armor said. "They did not dare to tell that it was gone. But we know."

"And," said Stark, "you will attack Kushat before the thaw, when they least expect you."

"You have a sharp mind, stranger. Yes. But the great wall will be hard to carry, even so. If I came, bearing in *my* hands the talisman of Ban Cruach. . . ."

He did not finish, but turned instead to Thord. "When you plundered the dead man's body, what did you find?"

"Nothing, Lord. A few coins, a knife, hardly worth the taking."

"And you, Eric John Stark. What did you take from the body?"

With perfect truth he answered, "Nothing."

"Thord," said the Lord Ciaran, "search him."

Thord came smiling up to Stark and ripped his jacket open.

With uncanny swiftness, the Earthman moved. The edge of one broad hand took Thord under the ear, and before the man's knees had time to sag Stark had caught his arm. He turned, crouching forward, and pitched Thord headlong through the door flap.

He straightened and turned again. His eyes held a feral glint. "The man has robbed me once," he said. "It is enough."

He heard Thord's men coming. Three of them tried to jam through the entrance at once, and he sprang at them. He made no sound. His fists did the talking for him, and then his feet, as he kicked the stunned barbarians back upon their leader.

"Now," he said to the Lord Ciaran, "will we talk as men?"

The man in armor laughed, a sound of pure enjoyment. It seemed that the gaze behind the mask studied Stark's savage face, and then lifted to greet the sullen Thord who came back into the shelter, his cheeks flushed crimson with rage.

"Go," said the Lord Ciaran. "The stranger and I will talk."

"But Lord," he protested, glaring at Stark, "it is not safe. . . ."

"My dark mistress looks after my safety," said Ciaran, stroking the axe across his knees. "Go."

Thord went.

The man in armor was silent then, the blind mask turned to Stark, who met that eyeless gaze and was silent also. And the bundle of rags in the shadows straightened slowly and became a tall old man with rusty hair and beard, through which peered craggy juts of bone and two bright, small points of fire, as though some wicked flame burned within him.

He shuffled over and crouched at the feet of the Lord Ciaran, watching the Earthman. And the man in armor leaned forward.

"I will tell you something, Eric John Stark. I am a bastard, but I come of the blood of kings. My name and rank I must make with my own hands. But I will set them high, and my name will ring in the Norlands!

"I will take Kushat. Who holds Kushat, holds Mars—and the power and the riches that lie beyond the Gates of Death!"

"I have seen them," said the old man, and his eyes blazed. "I have seen Ban Cruach the mighty. I have seen the temples and the palaces glitter in the ice. I have seen *Them*, the shining ones. Oh, I have seen them, the beautiful, hideous ones!"

He glanced sidelong at Stark, very cunning. "That is why Otar is mad, stranger. *He has seen.*"

A chill swept Stark. He too had seen, not with his own eyes but with the mind and memories of Ban Cruach, of a million years ago.

Then it had been no illusion, the fantastic vision opened to him by the talisman now hidden in his belt! If this old madman had seen. . . .

"What beings lurk beyond the Gates of Death I do not know," said Ciaran. "But my dark mistress will test their strength—and I think my red wolves will hunt them down, once they get a smell of plunder."

"The beautiful, terrible ones," whispered Otar. "And oh, the temples and the palaces, and the great towers of stone!"

"Ride with me, Stark," said the Lord Ciaran abruptly. "Yield up the talisman, and be the shield at my back. I have offered no other man that honor."

Stark asked slowly, "Why do you choose me?"

"We are of one blood, Stark, though we be strangers."

The Earthman's cold eyes narrowed. "What would your red wolves say to that? And what would Otar say? Look at him, already stiff with jealousy, and fear lest I answer, 'Yes'."

"I do not think you would be afraid of either of them."

"On the contrary," said Stark, "I am a prudent man." He paused. "There is one other thing. I will bargain with no man until I have looked into his eyes. Take off your helm, Ciaran—and then perhaps we will talk!"

Otar's breath made a snakelike hissing between his toothless gums, and the hands of the Lord Ciaran tightened on the haft of the axe.

"No!" he whispered. "That I can never do."

Otar rose to his feet, and for the first time Stark felt the full strength that lay in this strange old man.

"Would you look upon the face of destruction?" he thundered. "Do you ask for death? Do you think a thing is hidden behind a mask of steel without a reason, that you demand to see it?"

He turned. "My Lord," he said. "By tomorrow the last of the clans will have joined us. After that, we must march. Give this Earthman to Thord, for the time that remains—and you will have the talisman."

The blank, blind mask was unmoving, turned toward Stark, and the Earthman thought that from behind it came a faint sound that might have been a sigh.

Then. . . .

"Thord!" cried the Lord Ciaran, and lifted up the axe.

III

The flames leaped high from the fire in the windless gorge. Men sat around it in a great circle, the wild riders out of the mountain valleys of Mekh. They sat with the curbed and shivering eagerness of wolves around a dying quarry. Now and again their white teeth showed in a kind of silent laughter, and their eyes watched.

"He is strong," they whispered, one to the other. "He will live the night out, surely!"

On an outcrop of rock sat the Lord Ciaran, wrapped in a black cloak, holding the great axe in the crook of his arm. Beside him, Otar huddled in the snow.

Close by, the long spears had been driven deep and lashed together to make a scaffolding, and upon this frame was hung a man. A big man, iron-muscled and very lean, the bulk of his shoulders filling the space between the bending shafts. Eric John Stark of Earth, out of Mercury.

He had already been scourged without mercy. He sagged of his own weight between the spears, breathing in harsh sobs, and the trampled snow around him was spotted red.

Thord was wielding the lash. He had stripped off his own coat, and his body glistened with sweat in spite of the cold. He cut his victim with great care, making the long lash sing and crack. He was proud of his skill.

Stark did not cry out.

Presently Thord stepped back, panting, and looked at the Lord Ciaran. And the black helm nodded.

Thord dropped the whip. He went up to the big dark man and lifted his head by the hair.

"Stark," he said, and shook the head roughly. "Stranger!"

Eyes opened and stared at him, and Thord could not repress a slight shiver. It seemed that the pain and indignity had wrought some evil magic on this man he had ridden with, and thought he knew. He had seen exactly the same gaze in a big snow-cat caught in a trap, and he felt suddenly that it was not a man he spoke to, but a predatory beast.

"Stark," he said. "Where is the talisman of Ban Cruach?"

The Earthman did not answer.

Thord laughed. He glanced up at the sky, where the moons rode low and swift.

"The night is only half gone. Do you think you can last it out?"

The cold, cruel, patient eyes watched Thord. There was no reply.

Some quality of pride in that gaze angered the barbarian. It seemed to mock him, who was so sure of his ability to loosen a reluctant tongue.

"You think I cannot make you talk, don't you? You don't know me, stranger! You don't know Thord, who can make the rocks speak out if he will!"

He reached out with his free hand and struck Stark across the face.

It seemed impossible that anything so still could move so quickly. There was an ugly flash of teeth, and Thord's wrist was caught above the thumb-joint. He bellowed, and the iron jaws closed down, worrying the bone.

Quite suddenly, Thord screamed. Not for pain, but for panic. And the rows of watching men swayed forward, and even the Lord Ciaran rose up, startled.

"*Hark!*" ran the whispering around the fire. "Hark how he growls!"

Thord had let go of Stark's hair and was beating him about the head with his clenched fist. His face was white.

"Werewolf!" he screamed. "Let me go, beast-thing! Let me go!"

But the dark man clung to Thord's wrist, snarling, and did not hear. After a bit there came the dull crack of bone.

Stark opened his jaws. Thord ceased to strike him. He backed off slowly, staring at the torn flesh. Stark had sunk down to the length of his arms.

With his left hand, Thord drew his knife. The Lord Ciaran stepped forward. "Wait, Thord!"

"It is a thing of evil," whispered the barbarian. "Warlock. Werewolf. Beast."

He sprang at Stark.

The man in armor moved, very swiftly, and the great axe went whirling through the air. It caught Thord squarely where the cords of his neck ran into the shoulder—caught, and shore on through.

There was a silence in the valley.

The Lord Ciaran walked slowly across the trampled snow and took up his axe again.

"I will be obeyed," he said. "And I will not stand for fear, not of god, man, nor devil." He gestured toward Stark. "Cut him down. And see that he does not die."

He strode away, and Otar began to laugh.

From a vast distance, Stark heard that shrill, wild laughter. His mouth was full of blood, and he was mad with a cold fury.

A cunning that was purely animal guided his movements then. His head fell forward, and his body hung inert against the thongs. He might almost have been dead.

A knot of men came toward him. He listened to them. They were hesitant and afraid. Then, as he did not move, they plucked up courage and came closer, and one prodded him gently with the point of his spear.

"Prick him well," said another. "Let us be sure!"

The sharp point bit a little deeper. A few drops of blood welled out and joined the small red streams that ran from the weals of the lash. Stark did not stir.

The spearman grunted. "He is safe enough now."

Stark felt the knife blades working at the thongs. He waited. The rawhide snapped, and he was free.

He did not fall. He would not have fallen then if he had taken a death wound. He gathered his legs under him and sprang.

He picked up the spearman in that first rush and flung him into the fire. Then he began to run toward the place where the scaly mounts were herded, leaving a trail of blood behind him on the snow.

A man loomed up in front of him. He saw the shadow of a spear and swerved, and caught the haft in his two hands. He wrenched it free and struck down with the butt of it, and went on. Behind him he heard voices shouting and the beginning of turmoil.

The Lord Ciaran turned and came back, striding fast.

There were men before Stark now, many men, the circle of watchers breaking up because there had been nothing more to watch. He gripped the long spear. It was a good weapon, better than the flint-tipped stick with which the boy N'Chaka had hunted the giant lizard of the rocks.

His body curved into a half crouch. He voiced one cry, the challenging scream of a predatory killer, and went in among the men.

He did slaughter with that spear. They were not expecting attack. They were not expecting anything. Stark had sprung to life too quickly. And they were afraid of him. He could smell the fear on them. Fear not of a man like themselves, but of a creature less and more than man.

He killed, and was happy.

They fell away from him, the wild riders of Mekh. They were sure now that he was a demon. He raged among them with the bright spear, and they heard again that sound that should not have come from a human throat, and their superstitious terror rose and sent them scrambling out of his path, trampling on each other in childish panic.

He broke through, and now there was nothing between him and escape but two mounted men who guarded the herd.

Being mounted, they had more courage. They felt that even a warlock could not stand against their charge. They came at him as he ran, the padded feet of their beasts making a muffled drumming in the snow.

Without breaking stride, Stark hurled his spear.

It drove through one man's body and tumbled him off, so that he fell under his comrade's mount and fouled its legs. It staggered and reared up, hissing, and Stark fled on.

Once he glanced over his shoulder. Through the milling, shouting crowd of men he glimpsed a dark, mailed figure with a winged mask, going through the ruck with a loping stride and bearing a sable axe raised high for the throwing.

Stark was close to the herd now. And they caught his scent.

The Norland brutes had never liked the smell of him, and

now the reek of blood upon him was enough in itself to set them wild. They began to hiss and snarl uneasily, rubbing their reptilian flanks together as they wheeled around, staring at him with lambent eyes.

He rushed them, before they should quite decide to break. He was quick enough to catch one by the fleshy comb that served it for a forelock, held it with savage indifference to its squealing, and leaped to its back. Then he let it bolt, and as he rode it he yelled, a shrill brute cry that urged the creatures on to panic.

The herd broke, stampeding outward from its center like a bursting shell.

Stark was in the forefront. Clinging low to the scaly neck, he saw the men of Mekh scattered and churned and tramped into the snow by the flying pads. In and out of the shelters, kicking the brush walls down, lifting up their harsh reptilian voices, they went racketing through the camp, leaving behind them wreckage as of a storm. And Stark went with them.

He snatched a cloak from off the shoulders of some petty chieftain as he went by, and then, twisting cruelly on the fleshy comb, beating with his fist at the creature's head, he got his mount turned in the way he wanted it to go, down the valley.

He caught one last glimpse of the Lord Ciaran, fighting to hold one of the creatures long enough to mount, and then a dozen striving bodies surged around him, and Stark was gone.

The beast did not slacken pace. It was as though it thought it could outrun the alien, bloody thing that clung to its back. The last fringes of the camp shot by and vanished in the gloom, and the clean snow of the lower valley lay open before it. The creature laid its belly to the ground and went, the white spray spurting from its heels.

Stark hung on. His strength was gone now, run out suddenly with the battle-madness. He became conscious now that he was sick and bleeding, that his body was one cruel pain. In that moment, more than in the hours that had gone before, he hated the black leader of the clans of Mekh.

That flight down the valley became a sort of ugly dream. Stark was aware of rock walls reeling past, and then they seemed to widen away and the wind came out of nowhere like the stroke of a great hammer, and he was on the open moors again.

The beast began to falter and slow down. Presently it stopped.

Stark scooped up snow to rub on his wounds. He came near to fainting, but the bleeding stopped and after that the pain was numbed to a dull ache. He wrapped the cloak around him and urged the beast to go on, gently this time, patiently, and after it had breathed it obeyed him, settling into the shuffling pace it could keep up for hours.

He was three days on the moors. Part of the time he rode in a sort of stupor, and part of the time he was feverishly alert, watching the skyline. Frequently he took the shapes of thrusting rocks for riders, and found what cover he could until he was sure they did not move. He was afraid to dismount, for the beast had no bridle. When it halted to rest he remained upon its back, shaking, his brow beaded with sweat.

The wind scoured his tracks clean as soon as he made them. Twice, in the distance, he did see riders, and one of those times he burrowed into a tall drift and stayed there for several hours.

The ruined towers marched with him across the bitter land, lonely giants fifty miles apart. He did not go near them.

He knew that he wandered a good bit, but he could not help it, and it was probably his salvation. In those tortured badlands, riven by ages of frost and flood, one might follow a man on a straight track between two points. But to find a single rider lost in that wilderness was a matter of sheer luck, and the odds were with Stark.

One evening at sunset he came out upon a plain that sloped upward to a black and towering scarp, notched with a single pass.

The light was level and blood-red, glittering on the frosty rock so that it seemed the throat of the pass was aflame with evil fires. To Stark's mind, essentially primitive and stripped now of all its acquired reason, that narrow cleft appeared as the doorway to the dwelling place of demons as horrible as the fabled creatures that roam the Darkside of his native world.

He looked long at the Gates of Death, and a dark memory crept into his brain. Memory of that nightmare experience when the talisman had made him seem to walk into that frightful pass, not as Stark, but as Ban Cruach.

He remembered Otar's words—*I have seen Ban Cruach the mighty.* Was he still there beyond those darkling gates, fighting his unimagined war, alone?

Again, in memory, Stark heard the evil piping of the wind. Again, the shadow of a dim and terrible shape loomed up before him. . . .

He forced remembrance of that vision from his mind, by a great effort. He could not turn back now. There was no place to go.

His weary beast plodded on, and now Stark saw as in a dream that a great walled city stood guard before that awful Gate. He watched the city glide toward him through a crimson haze, and fancied he could see the ages clustered like birds around the towers.

He had reached Kushat, with the talisman of Ban Cruach still strapped in the bloodstained belt around his waist.

IV

He stood in a large square, lined about with huckster's stalls and the booths of wine-sellers. Beyond were buildings, streets, a city. Stark got a blurred impression of a grand and brooding darkness, bulking huge against the mountains, as bleak and proud as they, and quite as ancient, with many ruins and deserted quarters.

He was not sure how he had come there, but he was standing on his own feet, and someone was pouring sour wine into his mouth. He drank it greedily. There were people around him, jostling, chattering, demanding answers to their questions. A girl's voice said sharply, "Let him be! Can't you see he's hurt?"

Stark looked down. She was slim and ragged, with black hair and large eyes yellow as a cat's. She held a leather bottle in her hands. She smiled at him and said, "I'm Thanis. Will you drink more wine?"

"I will," said Stark, and did, and then said, "Thank you, Thanis." He put his hand on her shoulder, to steady himself. It was a supple shoulder, surprisingly strong. He liked the feel of it.

The crowd was still churning around him, growing larger, and now he heard the tramp of military feet. A small detachment of men in light armor pushed their way through.

A very young officer whose breastplate hurt the eye with brightness demanded to be told at once who Stark was and why he had come there.

"No one crosses the moors in winter," he said, as though that in itself were a sign of evil intent.

"The clans of Mekh are crossing them," Stark answered. "An army, to take Kushat—one, two days behind me."

The crowd picked that up. Excited voices tossed it back and forth, and clamored for more news. Stark spoke to the officer.

"I will see your captain, and at once."

"You'll see the inside of a prison, more likely!" snapped the young man. "What's this nonsense about the clans of Mekh?"

Stark regarded him. He looked so long and so curiously that the crowd began to snicker and the officer's beardless face flushed pink to the ears.

"I have fought in many wars," said Stark gently. "And long ago I learned to listen, when someone came to warn me of attack."

"Better take him to the captain, Lugh," cried Thanis. "It's our skins too, you know, if there is war."

The crowd began to shout. They were all poor folk, wrapped in threadbare cloaks or tattered leather. They had no love for the guards. And whether there was war or not, their winter had been long and dull, and they were going to make the most of this excitement.

"Take him, Lugh! Let him warn the nobles. Let them think how they'll defend Kushat and the Gates of Death, now that the talisman is gone!"

"That is a lie!" Lugh shouted. "And you know the penalty for telling it. Hold your tongues, or I'll have you all whipped." He gestured angrily at Stark. "See if he is armed."

One of the soldiers stepped forward, but Stark was quicker. He slipped the thong and let the cloak fall, baring his upper body.

"The clansmen have already taken everything I owned," he said. "But they gave me something, in return."

The crowd stared at the half healed stripes that scarred him, and there was a drawing in of breath.

The soldier picked up the cloak and laid it over the Earthman's shoulders. And Lugh said sullenly, "Come, then."

Stark's fingers tightened on Thanis' shoulder. "Come with me, little one," he whispered. "Otherwise, I must crawl."

She smiled at him and came. The crowd followed.

The captain of the guards was a fleshy man with a smell of wine about him and a face already crumbling apart though his hair was not yet grey. He sat in a squat tower above the square, and he observed Stark with no particular interest.

"You had something to tell," said Lugh. "Tell it."

Stark told them, leaving out all mention of Camar and the talisman. This was neither the time nor the man to hear that story. The captain listened to all he had to say about the gathering of the clans of Mekh, and then sat studying him with a bleary shrewdness.

"You have proof of all this?"

"These stripes. Their leader Ciaran ordered them laid on himself."

The captain sighed, and leaned back.

"Any wandering band of hunters could have scourged you," he said. "A nameless vagabond from the gods know where, and a lawless one at that, if I'm any judge of men—you probably deserved it."

He reached for wine, and smiled. "Look you, stranger. In the Norlands, no one makes war in the winter. And no one ever heard of Ciaran. If you hoped for a reward from the city, you overshot badly."

"The Lord Ciaran," said Stark, grimly controlling his anger, "will be battering at your gates within two days. And you will hear of him then."

"Perhaps. You can wait for him—in a cell. And you can leave Kushat with the first caravan after the thaw. We have enough rabble here without taking in more."

Thanis caught Stark by the cloak and held him back.

"*Sir*," she said, as though it were an unclean word. "I will vouch for the stranger."

The captain glanced at her. "You?"

"Sir, I am a free citizen of Kushat. According to law, I may vouch for him."

"If you scum of the Thieves' Quarter would practice the law as well as you prate it, we would have less trouble," growled the captain. "Very well, take the creature, if you want him. I don't suppose you've anything to lose."

Lugh laughed.

"Name and dwelling place," said the captain, and wrote them down. "Remember, he is not to leave the Quarter."

Thanis nodded. "Come," she said to Stark. He did not move, and she looked up at him. He was staring at the captain. His beard had grown in these last days, and his face was still scarred by Thord's blows and made wolfish with pain and fever. And now, out of this evil mask, his eyes were peering with a chill and terrible intensity at the soft-bellied man who sat and mocked him.

Thanis laid her hand on his rough cheek. "Come," she said. "Come and rest."

Gently she turned his head. He blinked and swayed, and she took him around the waist and led him unprotesting to the door.

There she paused, looking back.

"Sir," she said, very meekly, "news of this attack is being shouted through the Quarter now. If it *should* come, and it were known that you had the warning and did not pass it on. . . ." She made an expressive gesture, and went out.

Lugh glanced uneasily at the captain. "She's right, sir. If by chance the man did tell the truth. . . ."

The captain swore. "Rot. A rogue's tale. And yet. . . ." He scowled indecisively, and then reached for parchment. "After all, it's a simple thing. Write it up, pass it on, and let the nobles do the worrying."

His pen began to scratch.

Thanis took Stark by steep and narrow ways, darkling now in the afterglow, where the city climbed and fell again over the uneven rock. Stark was aware of the heavy smells of spices and unfamiliar foods, and the musky undertones of a million generations swarmed together to spawn and die in these crowded catacombs of slate and stone.

There was a house, blending into other houses, close under the loom of the great Wall. There was a flight of steps, hollowed deep with use, twisting crazily around outer corners.

There was a low room, and a slender man named Balin, vaguely glimpsed, who said he was Thanis' brother. There was a bed of skins and woven cloths.

Stark slept.

Hands and voices called him back. Strong hands shaking him, urgent voices. He started up growling, like an animal suddenly awaked, still lost in the dark mists of exhaustion. Balin swore, and caught his fingers away.

"What is this you have brought home, Thanis? By the gods, it snapped at me!"

Thanis ignored him. "Stark," she said. "Stark! Listen. Men are coming. Soldiers. They will question you. Do you hear me?"

Stark said heavily, "I hear."

"*Do not speak of Camar!*"

Stark got to his feet, and Balin said hastily, "Peace! The thing is safe. I would not steal a death warrant!"

His voice had a ring of truth. Stark sat down again. It was an effort to keep awake. There was clamor in the street below. It was still night.

Balin said carefully, "Tell them what you told the captain, nothing more. They will kill you if they know."

A rough hand thundered at the door, and a voice cried, "Open up!"

Balin sauntered over to lift the bar. Thanis sat beside Stark, her hand touching his. Stark rubbed his face. He had been shaved and washed, his wounds rubbed with salve. The belt was gone, and his bloodstained clothing. He realized only then that he was naked, and drew a cloth around him. Thanis whispered, "The belt is there on that peg, under your cloak."

Balin opened the door, and the room was full of men.

Stark recognized the captain. There were others, four of them, young, old, intermediate, annoyed at being hauled away from their beds and their gaming tables at this hour. The sixth man wore the jewelled cuirass of a noble. He had a nice, a kind face. Grey hair, mild eyes, soft cheeks. A fine man, but ludicrous in the trappings of a soldier.

"Is this the man?" he asked, and the captain nodded.

"Yes." It was his turn to say Sir.

Balin brought a chair. He had a fine flourish about him. He wore a crimson jewel in his left ear, and every line of him was quick and sensitive, instinct with mockery. His eyes were brightly cynical, in a face worn lean with years of merry sinning. Stark liked him.

He was a civilized man. They all were—the noble, the captain, the lot of them. So civilized that the origins of their culture were forgotten half an age before the first clay brick was laid in Babylon.

Too civilized, Stark thought. Peace had drawn their fangs and cut their claws. He thought of the wild clansmen coming fast across the snow, and felt a certain pity for the men of Kushat.

The noble sat down.

"This is a strange tale you bring, wanderer. I would hear it from your own lips."

Stark told it. He spoke slowly, watching every word, cursing the weariness that fogged his brain.

The noble, who was called Rogain, asked him questions. Where was the camp? How many men? What were the exact words of the Lord Ciaran, and who was he?

Stark answered, with meticulous care.

Rogain sat for some time lost in thought. He seemed worried and upset, one hand playing aimlessly with the hilt of his sword. A scholar's hand, without a callous on it.

"There is one thing more," said Rogain. "What business had you on the moors in winter?"

Stark smiled. "I am a wanderer by profession."

"Outlaw?" asked the captain, and Stark shrugged.

"Mercenary is a kinder word."

Rogain studied the pattern of stripes on the Earthman's dark skin. "Why did the Lord Ciaran, so-called, order you scourged?"

"I had thrashed one of his chieftains."

Rogain sighed and rose. He stood regarding Stark from under brooding brows, and at length he said, "It is a wild tale. I can't believe it—and yet, why should you lie?"

He paused, as though hoping that Stark would answer that and relieve him of worry.

Stark yawned. "The tale is easily proved. Wait a day or two."

"I will arm the city," said Rogain. "I dare not do otherwise. But I will tell you this." An astonishing unpleasant look came into his eyes. "If the attack does not come—if you have set a whole city by the ears for nothing—I will have you flayed alive and your body tumbled over the Wall for the carrion birds to feed on."

He strode out, taking his retinue with him. Balin smiled. "He will do it, too," he said, and dropped the bar.

Stark did not answer. He stared at Balin, and then at Thanis, and then at the belt hanging on the peg, in a curiously blank and yet penetrating fashion, like an animal that thinks its own thoughts. He took a deep breath. Then, as though he found the air clean of danger, he rolled over and went instantly to sleep.

Balin lifted his shoulders expressively. He grinned at Thanis. "Are you positive it's human?"

"He's beautiful," said Thanis, and tucked the cloths around him. "Hold your tongue." She continued to sit there, watching Stark's face as the slow dreams moved across it. Balin laughed.

It was evening again when Stark awoke. He sat up, stretching lazily. Thanis crouched by the hearthstone, stirring something savory in a blackened pot. She wore a red kirtle and a necklet of beaten gold, and her hair was combed out smooth and shining.

She smiled at him and rose, bringing him his own boots and trousers, carefully cleaned, and a tunic of leather tanned fine and soft as silk. Stark asked her where she got it.

"Balin stole it—from the baths where the nobles go. He said you might as well have the best." She laughed. "He had a devil of a time finding one big enough to fit you."

She watched with unashamed interest while he dressed. Stark said, "Don't burn the soup."

She put her tongue out at him. "Better be proud of that fine hide while you have it," she said. "There's no sign of attack."

Stark was aware of sounds that had not been there before— the pacing of men on the Wall above the house, the calling of the watch. Kushat was armed and ready—and his time was running out. He hoped that Ciaran had not been delayed on the moors.

Thanis said, "I should explain about the belt. When Balin undressed you, he saw Camar's name scratched on the inside of the boss. And, he can open a lizard's egg without harming the shell."

"What about you?" asked Stark.

She flexed her supple fingers. "I do well enough."

Balin came in. He had been seeking news, but there was little to be had.

"The soldiers are grumbling about a false alarm," he said. "The people are excited, but more as though they were playing a game. Kushat has not fought a war for centuries." He sighed. "The pity of it is, Stark, I believe your story. And I'm afraid."

Thanis handed him a steaming bowl. "Here—employ your tongue with this. Afraid, indeed! Have you forgotten the Wall? No one has carried it since the city was built. Let them attack!"

Stark was amused. "For a child, you know much concerning war."

"I knew enough to save your skin!" she flared, and Balin smiled.

"She has you there, Stark. And speaking of skins. . . ." He glanced up at the belt. "Or better, speaking of talismans, which we were not. How did you come by it?"

Stark told him. "He had a sin on his soul, did Camar. And—he was my friend."

Balin looked at him with deep respect. "You were a fool," he said. "Look you. The thing is returned to Kushat. Your promise is kept. There is nothing for you here but danger, and were I you I would not wait to be flayed, or slain, or taken in a quarrel that is not yours."

"Ah," said Stark softly, "but it is mine. The Lord Ciaran made it so." He, too, glanced at the belt. "What of the talisman?"

"Return it where it came from," Thanis said. "My brother is a better thief than Camar. He can certainly do that."

"No!" said Balin, with surprising force. "We will keep it, Stark and I. Whether it has power, I do not know. But if it has—I think Kushat will need it, and in strong hands."

Stark said somberly, "It has power, the Talisman. Whether for good or evil, I don't know."

They looked at him, startled. But a touch of awe seemed to repress their curiosity.

He could not tell them. He was, somehow, reluctant to tell anyone of that dark vision of what lay beyond the Gates of Death, which the talisman of Ban Cruach had lent him.

Balin stood up. "Well, for good or evil, at least the sacred relic of Ban Cruach has come home." He yawned. "I am going to bed. Will you come, Thanis, or will you stay and quarrel with our guest?"

"I will stay," she said, "and quarrel."

"Ah, well." Balin sighed puckishly. "Good night." He vanished into an inner room. Stark looked at Thanis. She had a warm mouth, and her eyes were beautiful, and full of light.

He smiled, holding out his hand.

The night wore on, and Stark lay drowsing. Thanis had opened the curtains. Wind and moonlight swept together into the room, and she stood leaning upon the sill, above the slumbering city. The smile that lingered in the corners of her mouth was sad and far-away, and very tender.

Stark stirred uneasily, making small sounds in his throat. His motions grew violent. Thanis crossed the room and touched him.

Instantly he was awake.

"Animal," she said softly. "You dream."

Stark shook his head. His eyes were still clouded, though not with sleep. "Blood," he said, "heavy in the wind."

"I smell nothing but the dawn," she said, and laughed.

Stark rose. "Get Balin. I'm going up on the Wall."

She did not know him now. "What is it, Stark? What's wrong?"

"Get Balin." Suddenly it seemed that the room stifled him. He caught up his cloak and Camar's belt and flung open the door, standing on the narrow steps outside. The moonlight caught in his eyes, pale as frost-fire.

Thanis shivered. Balin joined her without being called. He, too, had slept but lightly. Together they followed Stark up the rough-cut stair that led to the top of the Wall.

He looked southward, where the plain ran down from the mountains and spread away below Kushat. Nothing moved out there. Nothing marred the empty whiteness. But Stark said,

"They will attack at dawn."

V

They waited. Some distance away a guard leaned against the parapet, huddled in his cloak. He glanced at them incuriously. It was bitterly cold. The wind came whistling down through the Gates of Death, and below in the streets the watchfires shuddered and flared.

They waited, and still there was nothing.

Balin said impatiently, "How can you know they're coming?"

Stark shivered, a shallow rippling of the flesh that had nothing to do with cold, and every muscle of his body came alive. Phobos plunged downward. The moonlight dimmed and changed, and the plain was very empty, very still.

"They will wait for darkness. They will have an hour or so, between moonset and dawn."

Thanis muttered, "Dreams! Besides, I'm cold." She hesitated, and then crept in under Balin's cloak. Stark had gone away from her. She watched him sulkily where he leaned upon the stone. He might have been part of it, as dark and unstirring.

Deimos sank low toward the west.

Stark turned his head, drawn inevitably to look toward the cliffs above Kushat, soaring upward to blot out half the sky. Here, close under them, they seemed to tower outward in a curving mass, like the last wave of eternity rolling down, crested white with the ash of shattered worlds.

I have stood beneath those cliffs before. I have felt them leaning down to crush me, and I have been afraid.

He was still afraid. The mind that had poured its memories into that crystal lens had been dead a million years, but neither time nor death had dulled the terror that beset Ban Cruach in his journey through that nightmare pass.

He looked into the black and narrow mouth of the Gates of Death, cleaving the scarp like a wound, and the primitive apething within him cringed and moaned, oppressed with a sudden sense of fate.

He had come painfully across half a world, to crouch before the Gates of Death. Some evil magic had let him see forbidden things, had linked his mind in an unholy bond with the long-dead mind of one who had been half a god. These evil miracles had not been for nothing. He would not be allowed to go unscathed.

He drew himself up sharply then, and swore. He had left N'Chaka behind, a naked boy running in a place of rocks and sun on Mercury. He had become Eric John Stark, a man, and civilized. He thrust the senseless premonition from him, and turned his back upon the mountains.

Deimos touched the horizon. A last gleam of reddish light tinged the snow, and then was gone.

Thanis, who was half asleep, said with sudden irritation, "I do not believe in your barbarians. I'm going home." She thrust Balin aside and went away, down the steps.

The plain was now in utter darkness, under the faint, far Northern stars.

Stark settled himself against the parapet. There was a sort of timeless patience about him. Balin envied it. He would have liked to go with Thanis. He was cold and doubtful, but he stayed.

Time passed, endless minutes of it, lengthening into what seemed hours.

Stark said, "Can you hear them?"

"No."

"They come." His hearing, far keener than Balin's, picked up the little sounds, the vast inchoate rustling of an army on the move in stealth and darkness. Light-armed men, hunters, used to stalking wild beasts in the show. They could move softly, very softly.

"I hear nothing," Balin said, and again they waited.

The westering stars moved toward the horizon, and at length in the east a dim pallor crept across the sky.

The plain was still shrouded in night, but now Stark could make out the high towers of the King City of Kushat, ghostly and indistinct—the ancient, proud high towers of the rulers and their nobles, set above the crowded Quarters of merchants and artisans and thieves. He wondered who would be king in Kushat by the time this unrisen sun had set.

"You were wrong," said Balin, peering. "There is nothing on the plain."

Stark said, "Wait."

Swiftly now, in the thin air of Mars, the dawn came with a rush and a leap, flooding the world with harsh light. It flashed in cruel brilliance from sword-blades, from spearheads, from helmets and burnished mail, from the war-harness of beasts, glistened on bare russet heads and coats of leather, set the banners of the clans to burning, crimson and gold and green, bright against the snow.

There was no sound, not a whisper, in all the land.

Somewhere a hunting horn sent forth one deep cry to split the morning. Then burst out the wild skirling of the mountain pipes and the broken thunder of drums, and a wordless scream of exultation that rang back from the Wall of Kushat like the very voice of battle. The men of Mekh began to move.

Raggedly, slowly at first, then more swiftly as the press of warriors broke and flowed, the barbarians swept toward the city as water sweeps over a broken dam.

Knots and clumps of men, tall men running like deer, leaping, shouting, swinging their great brands. Riders, spurring their mounts until they fled belly down. Spears, axes, swordblades tossing, a sea of men and beasts, rushing, trampling, shaking the ground with the thunder of their going.

And ahead of them all came a solitary figure in black mail, riding a raking beast trapped all in black, and bearing a sable axe.

Kushat came to life. There was a swarming and a yelling in the streets, and soldiers began to pour up onto the Wall. A thin company, Stark thought, and shook his head. Mobs of citizens choked the alleys, and every rooftop was full. A troop of nobles went by, brave in their bright mail, to take up their post in the square by the great gate.

Balin said nothing, and Stark did not disturb his thoughts. From the look of him, they were dark indeed.

Soldiers came and ordered them off the the Wall. They went back to their own roof, where they were joined by Thanis. She was in a high state of excitement, but unafraid.

"Let them attack!" she said. "Let them break their spears against the Wall. They will crawl away again."

Stark began to grow restless. Up in their high emplacements, the big ballistas creaked and thrummed. The muted song of the bows became a wailing hum. Men fell, and were kicked off the ledges by their fellows. The blood-howl of the clans rang unceasing on the frosty air, and Stark heard the rap of scaling ladders against stone.

Thanis said abruptly, "What is that—that sound like thunder?"

"Rams," he answered. "They are battering the gate."

She listened, and Stark saw in her face the beginning of fear.

It was a long fight. Stark watched it hungrily from the roof all that morning. The soldiers of Kushat did bravely and well, but they were as folded sheep against the tall killers of the mountains. By noon the officers were beating the Quarters for men to replace the slain.

Stark and Balin went up again, onto the Wall.

The clans had suffered. Their dead lay in windrows under the Wall, amid the broken ladders. But Stark knew his barbarians. They had sat restless and chafing in the valley for many days, and now the battle-madness was on them and they were not going to be stopped.

Wave after wave of them rolled up, and was cast back, and came on again relentlessly. The intermittent thunder boomed still from the gates, where sweating giants swung the rams under cover of their own bowmen. And everywhere, up and down through the forefront of the fighting, rode the man in black armor, and wild cheering followed him.

Balin said heavily, "It is the end of Kushat."

A ladder banged against the stones a few feet away. Men swarmed up the rungs, fierce-eyed clansmen with laughter in their mouths. Stark was first at the head.

They had given him a spear. He spitted two men through with it and lost it, and a third man came leaping over the parapet. Stark received him into his arms.

Balin watched. He saw the warrior go crashing back, sweeping his fellows off the ladder. He saw Stark's face. He heard the sounds and smelled the blood and sweat of war, and he was sick to the marrow of his bones, and his hatred of the barbarians was a terrible thing.

Stark caught up a dead man's blade, and within ten minutes his arm was as red as a butcher's. And ever he watched the winged helm that went back and forth below, a standard to the clans.

By mid-afternoon the barbarians had gained the Wall in three places. They spread inward along the ledges, pouring up in a resistless tide, and the defenders broke. The rout became a panic.

"It's all over now," Stark said. "Find Thanis, and hide her."

Balin let fall his sword. "Give me the talisman," he whispered, and Stark saw that he was weeping. "Give it me, and I will go beyond the Gates of Death and rouse Ban Cruach from his sleep. And if he has forgotten Kushat, I will take his power into my own hands. I will fling wide the Gates of Death and loose destruction on the men of Mekh—or if the legends are all lies, then I will die."

He was like a man crazed. "Give me the talisman!"

Stark slapped him, carefully and without heat, across the face. "Get your sister, Balin. Hide her, unless you would be uncle to a red-haired brat."

He went then, like a man who has been stunned. Screaming women with their children clogged the ways that led inward from the Wall, and there was bloody work afoot on the rooftops and in the narrow alleys.

The gate was holding, still.

Stark forced his way toward the square. The booths of the hucksters were overthrown, the wine-jars broken and the red wine spilled. Beasts squealed and stamped, tired of their chafing harness, driven wild by the shouting and the smell of blood. The dead were heaped high where they had fallen from above.

They were all soldiers here, clinging grimly to their last foothold. The deep song of the rams shook the very stones. The iron-sheathed timbers of the gate gave back an answering scream, and toward the end all other sounds grew hushed. The nobles came down slowly from the Wall and mounted, and sat waiting.

There were fewer of them now. Their bright armor was dented and stained, and their faces had a pallor on them.

One last hammer-stroke of the rams.

With a bitter shriek the weakened bolts tore out, and the great gate was broken through.

The nobles of Kushat made their first, and final charge.

As soldiers they went up against the riders of Mekh, and as soldiers they held them until they died. Those that were left were borne back into the square, caught as in the crest of an avalanche. And first through the gates came the winged battle-mask of the Lord Ciaran, and the sable axe that drank men's lives where it hewed.

There was a beast with no rider to claim it, tugging at its head-rope. Stark swung onto the saddle pad and cut it free. Where the press was thickest, a welter of struggling brutes and men fighting knee to knee, there was the man in black armor, riding like a god, magnificent, born to war. Stark's eyes shone with a strange, cold light. He struck his heels hard into the scaly flanks. The beast plunged forward.

In and over and through, making the long sword sing. The beast was strong, and frightened beyond fear. It bit and trampled, and Stark cut a path for them, and presently he shouted above the din,

"Ho, there! *Ciaran!*"

The black mask turned toward him, and the remembered voice spoke from behind the barred slot, joyously.

"The wanderer. The wild man!"

Their two mounts shocked together. The axe came down in a whistling curve, and a red swordblade flashed to meet it. Swift, swift, a ringing clash of steel, and the blade was shattered and the axe fallen to the ground.

Stark pressed in.

Ciaran reached for his sword, but his hand was numbed by the force of that blow and he was slow, a split second. The hilt of Stark's weapon, still clutched in his own numbed grip, fetched him a stunning blow on the helm, so that the metal rang like a flawed bell.

The Lord Ciaran reeled back, only for a moment, but long enough. Stark grasped the war-mask and ripped it off, and got his hands around the naked throat.

He did not break that neck, as he had planned. And the Clansmen who had started in to save their leader stopped and did not move.

Stark knew now why the Lord Ciaran had never shown his face.

The throat he held was white and strong, and his hands around it were buried in a mane of red-gold hair that fell down over the shirt of mail. A red mouth passionate with fury, wonderful curving bone under sculptured flesh, eyes fierce and proud and tameless as the eyes of a young eagle, fire-blue, defying him, hating him. . . .

"By the gods," said Stark, very softly. "By the eternal gods!"

VI

A woman! And in that moment of amazement, she was quicker than he.

There was nothing to warn him, no least flicker of expression. Her two fists came up together between his outstretched arms and caught him under the jaw with a force that nearly snapped his neck. He went over backward, clean out of the saddle, and lay sprawled on the bloody stones, half stunned, the wind knocked out of him.

The woman wheeled her mount. Bending low, she took up the axe from where it had fallen, and faced her warriors, who were as dazed as Stark.

"I have led you well," she said. "I have taken you Kushat. Will any man dispute me?"

They knew the axe, if they did not know her. They looked from side to side uneasily, completely at a loss, and Stark, still gasping on the ground, thought that he had never seen anything as proud and beautiful as she was then in her black mail, with her bright hair blowing and her glance like blue lightning.

The nobles of Kushat chose that moment to charge. This strange unmasking of the Mekhish lord had given them time to rally, and now they thought that the Gods had wrought a miracle to help them. They found hope, where they had lost everything but courage.

"A wench!" they cried. "A strumpet of the camps. *A woman!*"

They howled it like an epithet, and tore into the barbarians.

She who had been the Lord Ciaran drove the spurs in deep, so that the beast leaped forward screaming. She went, and did not look to see if any had followed, in among the men of Kushat. And the great axe rose and fell, and rose again.

She killed three, and left two others bleeding on the stones, and not once did she look back.

The clansmen found their tongues.

"Ciaran! Ciaran!"

The crashing shout drowned out the sound of battle. As one man, they turned and followed her.

Stark, scrambling for his life underfoot, could not forbear smiling. Their childlike minds could see only two alternatives—to slay her out of hand, or to worship her. They had chosen to worship. He thought the bards would be singing of the Lord Ciaran of Mekh as long as there were men to listen.

He managed to take cover behind a wrecked booth, and presently make his way out of the square. They had forgotten him, for the moment. He did not wish to wait, just then, until they—or she—remembered.

She.

He still did not believe it, quite. He touched the bruise under his jaw where she had struck him, and thought of the lithe, swift strength of her, and the way she had ridden alone into battle. He remembered the death of Thord, and how she had kept her red wolves tamed, and he was filled with wonder, and a deep excitement.

He remembered what she had said to him once—*We are of one blood, though we be strangers.*

He laughed, silently, and his eyes were very bright.

The tide of war had rolled on toward the King City, where from the sound of it there was hot fighting around the castle. Eddies of the main struggle swept shrieking through the streets, but the rat-runs under the Wall were clear. Everyone had stampeded inward, the victims with the victors close on their heels. The short northern day was almost gone.

He found a hiding place that offered reasonable safety, and settled himself to wait.

Night came, but he did not move. From the sounds that reached him, the sacking of Kushat was in full swing. They were looting the richer streets first. Their upraised voices were thick with wine, and mingled with the cries of women. The reflection of many fires tinged the sky.

By midnight the sounds began to slacken, and by the second hour after the city slept, drugged with wine and blood and the weariness of battle. Stark went silently out into the streets, toward the King City.

According to the immemorial pattern of Martian city-states,

the castles of the king and the noble families were clustered together in solitary grandeur. Many of the towers were fallen now, the great halls open to the sky. Time had crushed the grandeur that had been Kushat, more fatally than the boots of any conqueror.

In the house of the king, the flamboys guttered low and the chieftains of Mekh slept with their weary pipers among the benches of the banquet hall. In the niches of the tall, carved portal, the guards nodded over their spears. They, too, had fought that day. Even so, Stark did not go near them.

Shivering slightly in the bitter wind, he followed the bulk of the massive walls until he found a postern door, half open as some kitchen knave had left it in his flight. Stark entered, moving like a shadow.

The passageway was empty, dimly lighted by a single torch. A stairway branched off from it, and he climbed that, picking his way by guess and his memories of similar castles he had seen in the past.

He emerged into a narrow hall, obviously for the use of servants. A tapestry closed the end, stirring in the chill draught that blew along the floor. He peered around it, and saw a massive, vaulted corridor, the stone walls panelled in wood much split and blackened by time, but still showing forth the wonderful carvings of beasts and men, larger than life and overlaid with gold and bright enamel.

From the corridor a single doorway opened—and Otar slept before it, curled on a pallet like a dog.

Stark went back down the narrow hall. He was sure that there must be a back entrance to the king's chambers, and he found the little door he was looking for.

From there on was darkness. He felt his way, stepping with infinite caution, and presently there was a faint gleam of light filtering around the edges of another curtain of heavy tapestry.

He crept toward it, and heard a man's slow breathing on the other side.

He drew the curtain back, a careful inch. The man was sprawled on a bench athwart the door. He slept the honest sleep of exhaustion, his sword in his hand, the stains of his day's work still upon him. He was alone in the small room. A door in the farther wall was closed.

Stark hit him, and caught the sword before it fell. The man grunted once and became utterly relaxed. Stark bound him with his own harness and shoved a gag in his mouth, and went on, through the door in the opposite wall.

The room beyond was large and high and full of shadows. A fire burned low on the hearth, and the uncertain light showed dimly the hangings and the rich stuffs that carpeted the floor, and the dark, sparse shapes of furniture.

Stark made out the lattice-work of a covered bed, let into the wall after the northern fashion.

She was there, sleeping, her red-gold hair the colour of the flames.

He stood a moment, watching her, and then, as though she sensed his presence, she stirred and opened her eyes.

She did not cry out. He had known that she would not. There was no fear in her. She said, with a kind of wry humor, "I will have a word with my guards about this."

She flung aside the covering and rose. She was almost as tall as he, white-skinned and very straight. He noted the long thighs, the narrow loins and magnificent shoulders, the small virginal breasts. She moved as a man moves, without coquetry. A long furred gown, that Stark guessed had lately graced the shoulders of the king, lay over a chair. She put it on.

"Well, wild man?"

"I have come to warn you." He hesitated over her name, and she said,

"My mother named me Ciara, if that seems better to you." She gave him her falcon's glance. "I could have slain you in the square, but now I think you did me a service. The truth would have come out sometime—better then, when they had no time to think about it." She laughed. "They will follow me now, over the edge of the world, if I ask them."

Stark said slowly, "Even beyond the Gates of Death?"

"Certainly, there. Above all, there!"

She turned to one of the tall windows and looked out at the

cliffs and the high notch of the pass, touched with greenish silver by the little moons.

"Ban Cruach was a great king. He came out of nowhere to rule the Norlands with a rod of iron, and men speak of him still as half a god. Where did he get his power, if not from beyond the Gates of Death? Why did he go back there at the end of his days, if not to hide away his secret? Why did he build Kushat to guard the pass forever, if not to hoard that power out of reach of all the other nations of Mars?

"Yes, Stark. My men will follow me. And if they do not, I will go alone."

"You are not Ban Cruach. Nor am I." He took her by the shoulders. "Listen, Ciara. You're already king in the Norlands, and half a legend as you stand. Be content."

"Content!" Her face was close to his, and he saw the blaze of it, the white intensity of ambition and an iron pride. "Are you content?" she asked him. "Have you ever been content?"

He smiled. "For strangers, we do know each other well. No. But the spurs are not so deep in me."

"The wind and the fire. One spends its strength in wandering, the other devours. But one can help the other. I made you an offer once, and you said you would not bargain unless you could look into my eyes. Look now!"

He did, and his hands upon her shoulders trembled.

"No," he said harshly. "You're a fool, Ciara. Would you be as Otar, mad with what you have seen?"

"Otar is an old man, and likely crazed before he crossed the mountains. Besides—I am not Otar."

Stark said somberly, "Even the bravest may break. Ban Cruach himself. . . ."

She must have seen the shadow of that horror in his eyes, for he felt her body tense.

"What of Ban Cruach? What do you know, Stark? Tell me!"

He was silent, and she went from him angrily.

"You have the talisman," she said. "That I am sure of. And if need be, I will flay you alive to get it!" She faced him across the room. "But whether I get it or not, I will go through the Gates of

Death. I must wait, now, until after the thaw. The warm wind will blow soon, and the gorges will be running full. But afterward, I will go, and no talk of fears and demons will stop me."

She began to pace the room with long strides, and the full skirts of the gown made a subtle whispering about her.

"You do not know," she said, in a low and bitter voice. "I was a girl-child, without a name. By the time I could walk, I was a servant in the house of my grandfather. The two things that kept me living were pride and hate. I left my scrubbing of floors to practice arms with the young boys. I was beaten for it every day, but every day I went. I knew even then that only force would free me. And my father was a king's son, a good man of his hands. His blood was strong in me. I learned."

She held her head very high. She had earned the right to hold it so.

She finished quietly, "I have come a long way. I will not turn back now."

"Ciara." Stark came and stood before her. "I am talking to you as a fighting man, an equal. There may be power behind the Gates of Death, I do not know. But this I have seen—madness, horror, an evil that is beyond our understanding.

"I think you will not accuse me of cowardice. And yet I would not go into that pass for all the power of all the kings of Mars!"

Once started, he could not stop. The full force of that dark vision of the talisman swept over him again in memory. He came closer to her, driven by the need to make her understand.

"Yes, I have the talisman! And I have had a taste of its purpose. I think Ban Cruach left it as a warning, so that none would follow him. I have seen the temples and the palaces glitter in the ice. I have seen the Gates of Death—*not with my own eyes, Ciara, but with his. With the eyes and the memories of Ban Cruach!*"

He had caught her again, his hands strong on her strong arms.

"Will you believe me, or must you see for yourself—the dreadful things that walk those buried streets, the shapes that rise from nowhere in the mists of the pass?"

Her gaze burned into his. Her breath was hot and sweet upon his lips, and she was like a sword between his hands, shining and unafraid.

"Give me the talisman. Let me see!"

He answered furiously, "You are mad. As mad as Otar." And he kissed her, in a rage, in a panic lest all that beauty be destroyed—a kiss as brutal as a blow, that left him shaken.

She backed away slowly, one step, and he thought she would have killed him. He said heavily:

"If you will see, you will. The thing is here."

He opened the boss and laid the crystal in her outstretched hand. He did not meet her eyes.

"Sit down. Hold the flat side against your brow."

She sat, in a great chair of carven wood. Stark noticed that her hand was unsteady, her face the colour of white ash. He was glad she did not have the axe where she could reach it. She did not play at anger.

For a long moment she studied the intricate lens, the incredible depository of a man's mind. Then she raised it slowly to her forehead.

He saw her grow rigid in the chair. How long he watched beside her he never knew. Seconds, an eternity. He saw her eyes turn blank and strange, and a shadow came into her face, changing it subtly, altering the lines, so that it seemed almost a stranger was peering through her flesh.

All at once, in a voice that was not her own, she cried out terribly, *"Oh gods of Mars!"*

The talisman dropped rolling to the floor, and Ciara fell forward into Stark's arms.

He thought at first that she was dead. He carried her to the bed, in an agony of fear that surprised him with its violence, and laid her down, and put his hand over her heart.

It was beating strongly. Relief that was almost a sickness swept over him. He turned, searching vaguely for wine, and saw the talisman. He picked it up and put it back inside the boss. A jewelled flagon stood on a table across the room. He took it and started back, and then, abruptly, there was a wild clamor in the hall outside and Otar was shouting Ciara's name, pounding on the door.

It was not barred. In another moment they would burst through, and he knew that they would not stop to enquire what he was doing there.

He dropped the flagon and went out swiftly, the way he had come. The guard was still unconscious. In the narrow hall beyond, Stark hesitated. A woman's voice was rising high above the tumult in the main corridor, and he thought he recognized it.

He went to the tapestry curtain and looked for the second time around its edge.

The lofty space was full of men, newly wakened from their heavy sleep and as nervous as so many bears. Thanis struggled in the grip of two of them. Her scarlet kirtle was torn, her hair flying in wild elf-locks, and her face was the face of a mad thing. The whole story of the doom of Kushat was written large upon it.

She screamed again and again, and would not be silenced.

"Tell her, the witch that leads you! Tell her that she is already doomed to death, with all her army!"

Otar opened up the door of Ciara's room.

Thanis surged forward. She must have fled through all that castle before she was caught, and Stark's heart ached for her.

"You!" she shrieked through the doorway, and poured out all the filth of the quarter upon Ciara's name. "Balin has gone to bring doom upon you! He will open wide the Gates of Death, and then you will die!—die!—*die!*"

Stark felt the shock of a terrible dread, as he let the curtain fall. Mad with hatred against conquerors, Balin had fulfilled his raging promise and had gone to fling open the Gates of Death.

Remembering his nightmare vision of the shining, evil ones whom Ban Cruach had long ago prisoned beyond those gates, Stark felt a sickness grow within him as he went down the stair and out the postern door.

It was almost dawn. He looked up at the brooding cliffs, and it seemed to him that the wind in the pass had a sound of laughter that mocked his growing dread.

He knew what he must do, if an ancient, mysterious horror was not to be released upon Kushat.

I may still catch Balin before he has gone too far! If I don't—

He dared not think of that. He began to walk very swiftly through the night streets, toward the distant, towering Gates of Death.

VII

It was past noon. He had climbed high toward the saddle of the pass. Kushat lay small below him, and he could see now the pattern of the gorges, cut ages deep in the living rock, that carried the spring torrents of the watershed around the mighty ledge on which the city was built.

The pass itself was channeled, but only by its own snows and melting ice. It was too high for a watercourse. Nevertheless, Stark thought, a man might find it hard to stay alive if he were caught there by the thaw.

He had seen nothing of Balin. The gods knew how many hours' start he had. Stark imagined him, scrambling wild-eyed over the rocks, driven by the same madness that had sent Thanis up into the castle to call down destruction on Ciara's head.

The sun was brilliant but without warmth. Stark shivered, and the icy wind blew strong. The cliffs hung over him, vast and sheer and crushing, and the narrow mouth of the pass was before him. He would go no farther. He would turn back, now.

But he did not. He began to walk forward, into the Gates of Death.

The light was dim and strange at the bottom of that cleft. Little veils of mist crept and clung between the ice and the rock, thickened, became more dense as he went farther and farther into the pass. He could not see, and the wind spoke with many tongues, piping in the crevices of the cliffs.

The steps of the Earthman slowed and faltered. He had known fear in his life before. But now he was carrying the burden of two men's terrors—Ban Cruach's, and his own.

He stopped, enveloped in the clinging mist. He tried to reason with himself—that Ban Cruach's fears had died a million years ago, that Otar had come this way and lived, and Balin had come also.

But the thin veneer of civilization sloughed away and left him with the naked bones of truth. His nostrils twitched to the smell of evil, the subtle unclean taint that only a beast, or one as close to it as he, can sense and know. Every nerve was a point of pain, raw with apprehension. An overpowering recognition of danger, hidden somewhere, mocking at him, made his very body change, draw in upon itself and flatten forward, so that when at last he went on again he was more like a four-footed thing than a man walking upright.

Infinitely wary, silent, moving surely over the ice and the tumbled rock, he followed Balin. He had ceased to think. He was going now on sheer instinct.

The pass led on and on. It grew darker, and in the dim uncanny twilight there were looming shapes that menaced him, and ghostly wings that brushed him, and a terrible stillness that was not broken by the eerie voices of the wind.

Rock and mist and ice. Nothing that moved or lived. And yet the sense of danger deepened, and when he paused the beating of his heart was like thunder in his ears.

Once, far away, he thought he heard the echoes of a man's voice crying, but he had no sight of Balin.

The pass began to drop, and the twilight deepened into a kind of sickly night.

On and down, more slowly now, crouching, slinking, heavily oppressed, tempted to snarl at boulders and tear at wraiths of fog. He had no idea of the miles he had travelled. But the ice was thicker now, the cold intense.

The rock walls broke off sharply. The mist thinned. The pallid darkness lifted to a clear twilight. He came to the end of the Gates of Death.

Stark stopped. Ahead of him, almost blocking the end of the pass, something dark and high and massive loomed in the thinning mists.

It was a great cairn, and upon it sat a figure, facing outward from the Gates of Death as though it kept watch over whatever country lay beyond.

The figure of a man in antique Martian armor.

After a moment, Stark crept toward the cairn. He was still almost all savage, torn between fear and fascination.

He was forced to scramble over the lower rocks of the cairn itself. Quite suddenly he felt a hard shock, and a flashing sensation of warmth that was somehow inside his own flesh, and not in any tempering of the frozen air. He gave a startled leap forward, and whirled, looking up into the face of the mailed figure with the confused idea that it had reached down and struck him.

It had not moved, of course. And Stark knew, with no need of anyone to tell him, that he looked into the face of Ban Cruach.

It was a face made for battles and for ruling, the bony ridges harsh and strong, the hollows under them worn deep with years. Those eyes, dark shadows under the rusty helm, had dreamed high dreams, and neither age nor death had conquered them.

And even in death, Ban Cruach was not unarmed.

Clad as for battle in his ancient mail, he held upright between his hands a mighty sword. The pommel was a ball of crystal large as a man's fist, that held within it a spark of intense brilliance. The little, blinding flame throbbed with its own force, and the sword-blade blazed with a white, cruel radiance.

Ban Cruach, dead but frozen to eternal changelessness by the bitter cold, sitting here upon his cairn for a million years and warding forever the inner end of the Gates of Death, as his ancient city of Kushat warded the outer.

Stark took two cautious steps closer to Ban Cruach, and felt again the shock and the flaring heat in his blood. He recoiled, satisfied.

The strange force in the blazing sword made an invisible barrier across the mouth of the pass, protected Ban Cruach himself. A barrier of short waves, he thought, of the type used in deep therapy, having no heat in themselves but increasing the heat in body cells by increasing their vibration. But these waves were stronger than any he had known before.

A barrier, a wall of force, closing the inner end of the Gates of Death. A barrier that was not designed against man.

Stark shivered. He turned from the sombre, brooding form of Ban Cruach and his eyes followed the gaze of the dead king, out beyond the cairn.

He looked across this forbidden land within the Gates of Death.

At his back was the mountain barrier. Before him, a handful of miles to the north, the terminus of the polar cap rose like a cliff of bluish crystal soaring up to touch the early stars. Locked in between those two titanic walls was a great valley of ice.

White and glimmering that valley was, and very still, and very beautiful, the ice shaped gracefully into curving domes and hollows. And in the center of it stood a dark tower of stone, a cyclopean bulk that Stark knew must go down an unguessable distance to its base on the bedrock. It was like the tower in which Camar had died. But this one was not a broken ruin. It loomed with alien arrogance, and within its bulk pallid lights flickered eerily, and it was crowned by a cloud of shimmering darkness.

It was like the tower of his dread vision, the tower that he had seen, not as Eric John Stark, but as Ban Cruach!

Stark's gaze dropped slowly from the evil tower to the curving ice of the valley. And the fear within him grew beyond all bounds.

He had seen that, too, in his vision. The glimmering ice, the domes and hollows of it. He had looked down through it at the city that lay beneath, and he had seen those who came and went in the buried streets.

Stark hunkered down. For a long while he did not stir.

He did not want to go out there. He did not want to go out from the grim, warning figure of Ban Cruach with his blazing sword, into that silent valley. He was afraid, afraid of what he might see if he went there and looked down through the ice, afraid of the final dread fulfillment of his vision.

But he had come after Balin, and Balin must be out there somewhere. He did not want to go, but he was himself, and he must.

He went, going very softly, out toward the tower of stone. And there was no sound in all that land.

The last of the twilight had faded. The ice gleamed, faintly luminous under the stars, and there was light beneath it, a soft radiance that filled all the valley with the glow of a buried moon.

Stark tried to keep his eyes upon the tower. He did not wish to look down at what lay under his stealthy feet.

Inevitably, he looked.

The temples and the palaces glittering in the ice. . . .

Level upon level, going down. Wells of soft light spanned with soaring bridges, slender spires rising, an endless variation of streets and crystal walls exquisitely patterned, above and below and overlapping, so that it was like looking down through a thousand giant snowflakes. A metropolis of gossamer and frost, fragile and lovely as a dream, locked in the clear, pure vault of the ice.

Stark saw the people of the city passing along the bright streets, their outlines blurred by the icy vault as things are half obscured by water. The creatures of vision, vaguely shining, infinitely evil.

He shut his eyes and waited until the shock and the dizziness left him. Then he set his gaze resolutely on the tower, and crept on, over the glassy sky that covered those buried streets.

Silence. Even the wind was hushed.

He had gone perhaps half the distance when the cry rang out.

It burst upon the valley with a shocking violence. *"Stark! Stark!"* The ice rang with it, curving ridges picked up his name and flung it back and forth with eerie crystal voices, and the echoes fled out whispering *Stark! Stark!* until it seemed that the very mountains spoke.

Stark whirled about. In the pallid gloom between the ice and the stars there was light enough to see the cairn behind him, and the dim figure atop it with the shining sword.

Light enough to see Ciara, and the dark knot of riders who had followed her through the Gates of Death.

She cried his name again. "Come back! Come back!"

The ice of the valley answered mockingly, *"Come back! Come back!"* and Stark was gripped with a terror that held him motionless.

She should not have called him. She should not have made a sound in that deathly place.

A man's hoarse scream rose above the flying echoes. The riders turned and fled suddenly, the squealing, hissing beasts crowding each other, floundering wildly on the rocks of the cairn, stampeding back into the pass.

Ciara was left alone. Stark saw her fight the rearing beast she rode and then flung herself out of the saddle and let it go. She came toward him, running, clad all in her black armor, the great axe swinging high.

"Behind you, Stark! Oh, gods of Mars!"

He turned then and saw them, coming out from the tower of stone, the pale, shining creatures that move so swiftly across the ice, so fleet and swift that no man living could outrun them.

He shouted to Ciara to turn back. He drew his sword and over his shoulder he cursed her in a black fury because he could hear her mailed feet coming on behind him.

The gliding creatures, sleek and slender, reedlike, bending, delicate as wraiths, their bodies shaped from northern rainbows of amethyst and rose—if they should touch Ciara, if their loathsome hands should touch her. . . .

Stark let out one raging catlike scream, and rushed them.

The opalescent bodies slipped away beyond his reach. The creatures watched him.

They had no faces, but they watched. They were eyeless but not blind, earless, but not without hearing. The inquisitive tendrils that formed their sensory organs stirred and shifted like the petals of ungodly flowers, and the color of them was the white frost-fire that dances on the snow.

"Go back, Ciara!"

But she would not go, and he knew that they would not have let her. She reached him, and they set their backs together. The shining ones ringed them round, many feet away across the ice, and watched the long sword and the great hungry axe, and there was something in the lissome swaying of their bodies that suggested laughter.

"You fool," said Stark. "You bloody fool."

"And you?" answered Ciara. "Oh, yes, I know about Balin. That mad girl, screaming in the palace—she told me, and you were seen from the wall, climbing to the Gates of Death. I tried to catch you."

"Why?"

She did not answer that. "They won't fight us, Stark. Do you think we could make it back to the cairn?"

"No. But we can try."

Guarding each others' backs, they began to walk toward Ban Cruach and the pass. If they could once reach the barrier, they would be safe.

Stark knew now what Ban Cruach's wall of force was built against. And he began to guess the riddle of the Gates of Death.

The shining ones glided with them, out of reach. They did not try to bar the way. They formed a circle around the man and woman, moving with them and around them at the same time, an endless weaving chain of many bodies shining with soft jewel tones of color.

They drew closer and closer to the cairn, to the brooding figure of Ban Cruach and his sword. It crossed Stark's mind that the creatures were playing with him and Ciara. Yet they had no weapons. Almost, he began to hope. . . .

From the tower where the shimmering cloud of darkness clung came a black crescent of force that swept across the ice-field like a sickle and gathered the two humans in.

Stark felt a shock of numbing cold that turned his nerves to ice. His sword dropped from his hand, and he heard Ciara's axe go down. His body was without strength, without feeling, dead.

He fell, and the shining ones glided in toward him.

VIII

Twice before in his life Stark had come near to freezing. It had been like this, the numbness and the cold. And yet it seemed that the dark force had struck rather at his nerve centers than at his flesh.

He could not see Ciara, who was behind him, but he heard the metallic clashing of her mail and one small, whispered cry, and he knew that she had fallen, too.

The glowing creatures surrounded him. He saw their bodies bending over him, the frosty tendrils of their faces writhing as though in excitement or delight.

Their hands touched him. Little hands with seven fingers, deft and frail. Even his numbed flesh felt the terrible cold of their touch, freezing as outer space. He yelled, or tried to, but they were not abashed.

They lifted him and bore him toward the tower, a company of them, bearing his heavy weight upon their gleaming shoulders.

He saw the tower loom high and higher still above him. The cloud of dark force that crowned it blotted out the stars. It became too huge and high to see at all, and then there was a low flat arch of stone close above his face, and he was inside.

Straight overhead—a hundred feet, two hundred, he could not tell—was a globe of crystal, fitted into the top of the tower as a jewel is held in a setting.

The air around it was shadowed with the same eerie gloom that hovered outside, but less dense, so that Stark could see the smouldering purple spark that burned within the globe, sending out its dark vibrations.

A globe of crystal, with a heart of sullen flame. Stark remembered the sword of Ban Cruach, and the white fire that burned in its hilt.

Two globes, the bright-cored and the dark. The sword of Ban Cruach touched the blood with heat. The globe of the tower deadened the flesh with cold. It was the same force, but at opposite ends of the spectrum.

Stark saw the cryptic controls of that glooming globe—a bank of them, on a wide stone ledge just inside the tower, close beside him. There were shining ones on that ledge tending those controls, and there were other strange and massive mechanisms there too.

Flying spirals of ice climbed up inside the tower, spanning the great stone well with spidery bridges, joining icy galleries. In some of those galleries, Stark vaguely glimpsed rigid, gleaming figures like statues of ice, but he could not see them clearly as he was carried on.

He was being carried downward. He passed slits in the wall, and knew that the pallid lights he had seen through them were the moving bodies of the creatures as they went up and down these high-flung, icy bridges. He managed to turn his head to look down, and saw what was beneath him.

The well of the tower plunged down a good five hundred feet to bedrock, widening as it went. The web of ice-bridges and the spiral ways went down as well as up, and the creatures that carried him were moving smoothly along a transparent ribbon of ice no more than a yard in width, suspended over that terrible drop.

Stark was glad that he could not move just then. One instinctive start of horror would have thrown him and his bearers to the rock below, and would have carried Ciara with them.

Down and down, gliding in utter silence along the descending spiral ribbon. The great glooming crystal grew remote above him. Ice was solid now in the slots of the walls. He wondered if they had brought Balin this way.

There were other openings, wide arches like the one they had brought their captives through, and these gave Stark brief glimpses of broad avenues and unguessable buildings, shaped from the pellucid ice and flooded with the soft radiance that was like eerie moonlight.

At length, on what Stark took to be the third level of the city, the creatures bore him through one of these archways, into the streets beyond.

Below him now was the translucent thickness of ice that formed the floor of this level and the roof of the level beneath. He could see the blurred tops of delicate minarets, the clustering roofs that shone like chips of diamond.

Above him was an ice roof. Elfin spires rose toward it, delicate as needles. Lacy battlements and little domes, buildings star-shaped, wheel-shaped, the fantastic, lovely shapes of snow-crystals, frosted over with a sparkling foam of light.

The people of the city gathered along the way to watch, a living, shifting rainbow of amethyst and rose and green, against the pure blue-white. And there was no least whisper of sound anywhere.

For some distance they went through a geometric maze of streets. And then there was a cathedral-like building all arched and spired, standing in the center of a twelve-pointed plaza. Here they turned, and bore their captives in.

Stark saw a vaulted roof, very slim and high, etched with a glittering tracery that might have been carving of an alien sort, delicate as the weavings of spiders. The feet of his bearers were silent on the icy paving.

At the far end of the long vault sat seven of the shining ones in high seats marvellously shaped from the ice. And before them, grey-faced, shuddering with cold and not noticing it, drugged with a sick horror, stood Balin. He looked around once, and did not speak.

Stark was set on his feet, with Ciara beside him. He saw her face, and it was terrible to see the fear in her eyes, that had never shown fear before.

He himself was learning why men went mad beyond the Gates of Death.

Chill, dreadful fingers touched him expertly. A flash of pain drove down his spine, and he could stand again.

The seven who sat in the high seats were motionless, their bright tendrils stirring with infinite delicacy as though they studied the three humans who stood before them.

Stark thought he could feel a cold, soft fingering of his brain. It came to him that these creatures were probably telepaths. They lacked organs of speech, and yet they must have some efficient means of communications. Telepathy was not uncommon among the many races of the Solar System, and Stark had had experience with it before.

He forced his mind to relax. The alien impulse was instantly stronger. He sent out his own questing thought and felt it brush the edges of a consciousness so utterly foreign to his own that he knew he could never probe it, even had he had the skill.

He learned one thing—that the shining faceless ones looked upon him with equal horror and loathing. They recoiled from the unnatural human features, and most of all, most strongly, they abhorred the warmth of human flesh. Even the infinitesimal amount of heat radiated by their half-frozen human bodies caused the ice-folk discomfort.

Stark marshalled his imperfect abilities and projected a mental question to the seven.

"What do you want of us?"

The answer came back, faint and imperfect, as though the gap between their alien minds was almost too great to bridge. And the answer was one word.

"Freedom!"

Balin spoke suddenly. He voiced only a whisper, and yet the sound was shockingly loud in that crystal vault.

"They have asked me already. Tell them no, Stark! Tell them no!"

He looked at Ciara then, a look of murderous hatred. "If you turn them loose upon Kushat, I will kill you with my own hands before I die."

Stark spoke again, silently, to the seven. "I do not understand."

Again the struggling, difficult thought. "We are the old race, the kings of the glacial ice. Once we held all the land beyond the mountains, outside the pass you call the Gates of Death."

Stark had seen the ruins of the towers out on the moors. He knew how far their kingdom had extended.

"We *controlled* the ice, far outside the polar cap. Our towers blanketed the land with the dark force drawn from Mars itself, from the magnetic field of the planet. That radiation bars out heat, from the Sun, and even from the awful winds that blow warm from the south. So there was never any thaw. Our cities were many, and our race was great.

"Then came Ban Cruach, from the south. . . .

"He waged a war against us. He learned the secret of the crystal globes, and learned how to reverse their force and use it against us. He, leading his army, destroyed our towers one by one, and drove us back. . . .

"Mars needed water. The outer ice was melted, our lovely cities crumbled to nothing, so that creatures like Ban Cruach might have water! And our people died.

"We retreated at the last, to this our ancient polar citadel behind the Gates of Death. Even here, Ban Cruach followed.

He destroyed even this tower once, at the time of the thaw. But this city is founded in polar ice—and only the upper levels were harmed. Even Ban Cruach could not touch the heart of the eternal polar cap of Mars!

"When he saw that he could not destroy us utterly, he set himself in death to guard the Gates of Death with his blazing sword, that we might never again reclaim our ancient dominion.

"That is what we mean when we ask for freedom. We ask that you take away the sword of Ban Cruach, so that we may once again go out through the Gates of Death!"

Stark cried aloud, hoarsely, "No!"

He knew the barren deserts of the south, the wastes of red dust, the dead sea bottoms—the terrible thirst of Mars, growing greater with every year of the million that had passed since Ban Cruach locked the Gates of Death.

He knew the canals, the pitiful waterways that were all that stood between the people of Mars and extinction. He remembered the yearly release from death when the spring thaw brought the water rushing down from the north.

He thought of these cold creatures going forth, building again their great towers of stone, sheathing half a world in ice that would never melt. He thought of the people of Jekkara and Valkis and Barrakesh, of the countless cities of the south, watching for the flood that did not come, and falling at last to mingle their bodies with the blowing dust.

He said again, "No. Never."

The distant thought-voice of the seven spoke, and this time the question was addressed to Ciara.

Stark saw her face. She did not know the Mars he knew, but she had memories of her own—the mountain-valleys of Mekh, the moors, the snowy gorges. She looked at the shining ones in their high seats, and said,

"If I take that sword, it will be to use it against you as Ban Cruach did!"

Stark knew that the seven had understood the thought behind her words. He felt that they were amused.

"The secret of that sword was lost a million years ago, the day Ban Cruach died. Neither you nor anyone now knows how to use it as he did. But the sword's radiations of warmth still lock us here.

"We cannot approach that sword, for its vibrations of heat slay us if we do. But you warm-bodied ones can approach it. And you will do so, and take it from its place. *One of you will take it!*"

They were very sure of that.

"We can see, a little way, into your evil minds. Much we do not understand. But—the mind of the large man is full of the woman's image, and the mind of the woman turns to him. Also, there is a link between the large man and the small man, less strong, but strong enough."

The thought-voice of the seven finished, "The large man will take away the sword for us because he must—to save the other two."

Ciara turned to Stark. "They cannot force you, Stark. Don't let them. No matter what they do to me, don't let them!"

Balin stared at her with a certain wonder. "You would die, to protect Kushat?"

"Not Kushat alone, though its people too are human," she said, almost angrily. "There are my red wolves—a wild pack, but my own. And others." She looked at Balin. "What do *you* say? Your life against the Norlands?"

Balin made an effort to lift his head as high as hers, and the red jewel flashed in his ear. He was a man crushed by the falling of his world, and terrified by what his mad passion had led him into, here beyond the Gates of Death. But he was not afraid to die.

He said so, and even Ciara knew that he spoke the truth.

But the seven were not dismayed. Stark knew that when their thought-voice whispered in his mind, "It is not death alone you humans have to fear, but the manner of your dying. You shall see that, before you choose."

Swiftly, silently, those of the ice-folk who had borne the captives into the city came up from behind, where they had stood withdrawn and waiting. And one of them bore a crystal rod like a sceptre, with a spark of ugly purple burning in the globed end.

Stark leaped to put himself between them and Ciara. He struck out, raging, and because he was almost as quick as they, he caught one of the slim luminous bodies between his hands.

The utter coldness of that alien flesh burned his hands as frost will burn. Even so, he clung on, snarling, and saw the tendrils writhe and stiffen as though in pain.

Then, from the crystal rod, a thread of darkness spun itself to touch his brain with silence, and the cold that lies between the worlds.

He had no memory of being carried once more through the shimmering streets of that elfin, evil city, back to the stupendous well of the tower, and up along the spiral path of ice that soared those dizzy hundreds of feet from bedrock to the glooming crystal globe. But when he again opened his eyes, he was lying on the wide stone ledge at ice-level.

Beside him was the arch that led outside. Close above his head was the control bank that he had seen before.

Ciara and Balin were there also, on the ledge. They leaned stiffly against the stone wall beside the control bank, and facing them was a squat, round mechanism from which projected a sort of wheel of crystal rods.

Their bodies were strangely rigid, but their eyes and minds were awake. Terribly awake. Stark saw their eyes, and his heart turned within him.

Ciara looked at him. She could not speak, but she had no need to. *No matter what they do to me. . . .*

She had not feared the swordsmen of Kushat. She had not feared her red wolves, when he unmasked her in the square. She was afraid now. But she warned him, ordered him not to save her.

They cannot force you. Stark! Don't let them.

And Balin, too, pleaded with him for Kushat.

They were not alone on the ledge. The ice-folk clustered there, and out upon the flying spiral pathway, on the narrow bridges and the spans of fragile ice, they stood in hundreds watching, eyeless, faceless, their bodies drawn in rainbow lines across the dimness of the shaft.

Stark's mind could hear the silent edges of their laughter. Secret, knowing laughter, full of evil, full of triumph, and Stark was filled with a corroding terror.

He tried to move, to crawl toward Ciara standing like a carven image in her black mail. He could not.

Again her fierce, proud glance met his. And the silent laughter of the ice-folk echoed in his mind, and he thought it very strange that in this moment, now, he should realize that there had never been another woman like her on all of the worlds of the Sun.

The fear she felt was not for herself. It was for him.

Apart from the multitudes of the ice-folk, the group of seven stood upon the ledge. And now their thought-voice spoke to Stark, saying, "Look about you. Behold the men who have come before you through the Gates of Death!"

Stark raised his eyes to where their slender fingers pointed, and saw the icy galleries around the tower, saw more clearly the icy statues in them that he had only glimpsed before.

Men, set like images in the galleries. Men whose bodies were sheathed in a glittering mail of ice, sealing them forever. Warriors, nobles, fanatics and thieves—the wanderers of a million years who had dared to enter this forbidden valley, and had remained forever.

He saw their faces, their tortured eyes wide open, their features frozen in the agony of a slow and awful death.

"They refused us," the seven whispered. "They would not take away the sword. And so they died, as this woman and this man will die, unless you choose to save them.

"We will show you, human, how they died!"

One of the ice-folk bent and touched the squat, round mechanism that faced Balin and Ciara. Another shifted the pattern of control on the master-bank.

The wheel of crystal rods on that squat mechanism began to turn. The rods blurred, became a disc that spun faster and faster.

High above in the top of the tower the great globe brooded, shrouded in its cloud of shimmering darkness. The disc became a whirling blur. The glooming shadow of the globe deepened, co-alesced. It began to lengthen and descend, stretching itself down toward the spinning disc.

The crystal rods of the mechanism drank the shadow in. And out of that spinning blur there came a subtle weaving of threads of darkness, a gossamer curtain winding around Ciara and Balin so that their outlines grew ghostly and the pallor of their flesh was as the pallor of snow at night.

And still Stark could not move.

The veil of darkness began to sparkle faintly. Stark watched it, watched the chill motes brighten, watched the tracery of frost whiten over Ciara's mail, touch Balin's dark hair with silver.

Frost. Bright, sparkling, beautiful, a halo of frost around their bodies. A dust of splintered diamond across their faces, an aureole of brittle light to crown their heads.

Frost. Flesh slowly hardening in marbly whiteness, as the cold slowly increased. And yet their eyes still lived, and saw, and understood.

The thought-voice of the seven spoke again.

"You have only minutes now to decide! Their bodies cannot endure too much, and live again. Behold their eyes, and how they suffer!

"Only minutes, human! Take away the sword of Ban Cruach! Open for us the Gates of Death, and we will release these two, alive."

Stark felt again the flashing stab of pain along his nerves, as one of the shining creatures moved behind him. Life and feeling came back into his limbs.

He struggled to his feet. The hundreds of the ice-folk on the bridges and galleries watched him in an eager silence.

He did not look at them. His eyes were on Ciara's. And now, her eyes pleaded.

"Don't, Stark! Don't barter the life of the Norlands for me!"

The thought-voice beat at Stark, cutting into his mind with cruel urgency.

"Hurry, human! They are already beginning to die. Take away the sword, and let them live!"

Stark turned. He cried out, in a voice that made the icy bridges tremble:

"I will take the sword!"

He staggered out, then. Out through the archway, across the ice, toward the distant cairn that blocked the Gates of Death.

IX

Across the glowing ice of the valley Stark went at a stumbling run that grew swifter and more sure as his cold-numbed body began to regain its functions. And behind him, pouring out of the tower to watch, came the shining ones.

They followed after him, gliding lightly. He could sense their excitement, the cold, strange ecstasy of triumph. He knew that already they were thinking of the great towers of stone rising again above the Norlands, the crystal cities still and beautiful under the ice, all vestige of the ugly citadels of man gone and forgotten.

The seven spoke once more, a warning.

"If you turn toward us with the sword, the woman and the man will die. And you will die as well. For neither you nor any other can now use the sword as a weapon of offense."

Stark ran on. He was thinking then only of Ciara, with the frost-crystals gleaming on her marble flesh and her eyes full of mute torment.

The cairn loomed up ahead, dark and high. It seemed to Stark that the brooding figure of Ban Cruach watched him coming with those shadowed eyes beneath the rusty helm. The great sword blazed between those dead, frozen hands.

The ice-folk had slowed their forward rush. They stopped and waited, well back from the cairn.

Stark reached the edge of tumbled rock. He felt the first warm flare of the force-waves in his blood, and slowly the chill began to creep out from his bones. He climbed, scrambling upward over the rough stones of the cairn.

Abruptly, then, at Ban Cruach's feet, he slipped and fell. For a second it seemed that he could not move.

His back was turned toward the ice-folk. His body was bent forward, and shielded so, his hands worked with feverish speed.

From his cloak he tore a strip of cloth. From the iron boss he took the glittering lens, the talisman of Ban Cruach. Stark laid the lens against his brow, and bound it on.

The remembered shock, the flood and sweep of memories that were not his own. The mind of Ban Cruach thundering its warn-

ing, its hard-won knowledge of an ancient, epic war. . . .

He opened his own mind wide to receive those memories. Before he had fought against them. Now he knew that they were his one small chance in this swift gamble with death. Two things only of his own he kept firm in that staggering tide of another man's memories. Two names—Ciara and Balin.

He rose up again. And now his face had a strange look, a curious duality. The features had not changed, but somehow the lines of the flesh had altered subtly, so that it was almost as though the old unconquerable king himself had risen again in battle.

He mounted the last step or two and stood before Ban Cruach. A shudder ran through him, a sort of gathering and settling of the flesh, as though Stark's being had accepted the stranger within it. His eyes, cold and pale as the very ice that sheathed the valley, burned with a cruel light.

He reached and took the sword, out of the frozen hands of Ban Cruach.

As though it were his own, he knew the secret of the metal rings that bound its hilt, below the ball of crystal. The savage throb of the invisible radiation beat in his quickening flesh. He was warm again, his blood running swiftly, his muscles sure and strong. He touched the rings and turned them.

The fan-shaped aura of force that had closed the Gates of Death narrowed in, and as it narrowed it leaped up from the blade of the sword in a tongue of pale fire, faintly shimmering, made visible now by the full focus of its strength.

Stark felt the wave of horror bursting from the minds of the ice-folk as they perceived what he had done. And he laughed.

His bitter laughter rang harsh across the valley as he turned to face them, and he heard in his brain the shuddering, silent shriek that went up from all that gathered company. . . .

"Ban Cruach! Ban Cruach has returned!"

They had touched his mind. They knew.

He laughed again, and swept the sword in a flashing arc, and watched the long bright blade of force strike out more terrible than steel, against the rainbow bodies of the shining ones.

They fell. Like flowers under a scythe they fell, and all across the ice the ones who were yet untouched turned about in their hundreds and fled back toward the tower.

Stark came leaping down the cairn, the talisman of Ban Cruach bound upon his brow, the sword of Ban Cruach blazing in his hand.

He swung that awful blade as he ran. The force-beam that sprang from it cut through the press of creatures fleeing before him, hampered by their own numbers as they crowded back through the archway.

He had only a few short seconds to do what he had to do.

Rushing with great strides across the ice, spurning the withered bodies of the dead. . . . And then, from the glooming darkness that hovered around the tower of stone, the black cold beam struck down.

Like a coiling whip it lashed him. The deadly numbness invaded the cells of his flesh, ached in the marrow of his bones. The bright force of the sword battled the chill invaders, and a corrosive agony tore at Stark's inner body where the antipathetic radiations waged war.

His steps faltered. He gave one hoarse cry of pain, and then his limbs failed and he went heavily to his knees.

Instinct only made him cling to the sword. Waves of blinding anguish racked him. The coiling lash of darkness encircled him, and its touch was the abysmal cold of outer space, striking deep into his heart.

Hold the sword close, hold it closer, like a shield. The pain is great, but I will not die unless I drop the sword.

Ban Cruach the mighty had fought this fight before.

Stark raised the sword again, close against his body. The fierce pulse of its brightness drove back the cold. Not far, for the freezing touch was very strong. But far enough so that he could rise again and stagger on.

The dark force of the tower writhed and licked about him. He could not escape it. He slashed it in a blind fury with the blazing sword, and where the forces met a flicker of lightning leaped in the air, but it would not be beaten back.

He screamed at it, a raging cat-cry that was all Stark, all primitive fury at the necessity of pain. And he forced himself to run, to drag his tortured body faster across the ice. *Because Ciara is dying, because the dark cold wants me to stop. . . .*

The ice-folk jammed and surged against the archway, in a panic hurry to take refuge far below in their many-levelled city. He raged at them, too. They were part of the cold, part of the pain. Because of them Ciara and Balin were dying. He sent the blade of force lancing among them, his hatred rising full tide to join the hatred of Ban Cruach that lodged in his mind.

Stab and cut and slash with the long terrible beam of brightness. They fell and fell, the hideous shining folk, and Stark sent the light of Ban Cruach's weapon sweeping through the tower itself, through the openings that were like windows in the stone.

Again and again, stabbing through those open slits as he ran. And suddenly the dark beam of force ceased to move. He tore out of it, and it did not follow him, remaining stationary as though fastened to the ice.

The battle of forces left his flesh. The pain was gone. He sped on to the tower.

He was close now. The withered bodies lay in heaps before the arch. The last of the ice-folk had forced their way inside. Holding the sword level like a lance, Stark leaped in through the arch, into the tower.

The shining ones were dead where the destroying warmth had touched them. The flying spiral ribbons of ice were swept clean of them, the arching bridges and the galleries of that upper part of the tower.

They were dead along the ledge, under the control bank. They were dead across the mechanism that spun the frosty doom around Ciara and Balin. The whirling disc still hummed.

Below, in that stupendous well, the crowding ice-folk made a seething pattern of color on the narrow ways. But Stark turned his back on them and ran along the ledge, and in him was the heavy knowledge that he had come too late.

The frost had thickened around Ciara and Balin. It encrusted them like stiffened lace, and now their flesh was overlaid with a diamond shell of ice.

Surely they could not live!

He raised the sword to smite down at the whirring disc, to smash it, but there was no need. When the full force of that concentrated beam struck it, meeting the focus of shadow that it held, there was a violent flare of light and a shattering of crystal. The mechanism was silent.

The glooming veil was gone from around the ice-shelled man and woman. Stark forgot the creatures in the shaft below him. He turned the blazing sword full upon Ciara and Balin.

It would not affect the thin covering of ice. If the woman and the man were dead, it would not affect their flesh, any more than it had Ban Cruach's. But if they lived, if there was still a spark, a flicker beneath that frozen mail, the radiation would touch their blood with warmth, start again the pulse of life in their bodies.

He waited, watching Ciara's face. It was still as marble, and as white.

Something—instinct, or the warning mind of Ban Cruach that had learned a million years ago to beware the creatures of the ice—made him glance behind him.

Stealthy, swift and silent, up the winding ways they came. They had guessed that he had forgotten them in his anxiety. The sword was turned away from them now, and if they could take him from behind, stun him with the chill force of the sceptre-like rods they carried. . . .

He slashed them with the sword. He saw the flickering beam go down and down the shaft, saw the bodies fall like drops of rain, rebounding here and there from the flying spans and carrying the living with them.

He thought of the many levels of the city. He thought of all the countless thousands that must inhabit them. He could hold them off in the shaft as long as he wished if he had no other need for the sword. But he knew that as soon as he turned his back they would be upon him again, and if he should once fall. . . .

He could not spare a moment, or a chance.

He looked at Ciara, not knowing what to do, and it seemed to him that the sheathing frost had melted, just a little, around her face.

Desperately, he struck down again at the creatures in the shaft, and then the answer came to him.

He dropped the sword. The squat, round mechanism was beside him, with its broken crystal wheel. He picked it up.

It was heavy. It would have been heavy for two men to lift, but Stark was a driven man. Grunting, swaying with the effort, he lifted it and let it fall, out and down.

Like a thunderbolt it struck among those slender bridges, the spiderweb of icy strands that spanned the shaft. Stark watched it go, and listened to the brittle snapping of the ice, the final crashing of a million shards at the bottom far below.

He smiled, and turned again to Ciara, picking up the sword.

It was hours later. Stark walked across the glowing ice of the valley, toward the cairn. The sword of Ban Cruach hung at his side. He had taken the talisman and replaced it in the boss, and he was himself again.

Ciara and Balin walked beside him. The color had come back into their faces, but faintly, and they were still weak enough to be glad of Stark's hands to steady them.

At the foot of the cairn they stopped, and Stark mounted it alone.

He looked for a long moment into the face of Ban Cruach. Then he took the sword, and carefully turned the rings upon it so that the radiation spread out as it had before, to close the Gates of Death.

Almost reverently, he replaced the sword in Ban Cruach's hands. Then he turned and went down over the tumbled stones.

The shimmering darkness brooded still over the distant tower. Underneath the ice, the elfin city still spread downward. The shining ones would rebuild their bridges in the shaft, and go on as they had before, dreaming their cold dreams of ancient power.

But they would not go out through the Gates of Death. Ban Cruach in his rusty mail was still lord of the pass, the warder of the Norlands.

Stark said to the others, "Tell the story in Kushat. Tell it through the Norlands, the story of Ban Cruach and why he guards the Gates of Death. Men have forgotten. And they should not forget."

They went out of the valley then, the two men and the woman. They did not speak again, and the way out through the pass seemed endless.

Some of Ciara's chieftains met them at the mouth of the pass above Kushat. They had waited there, ashamed to return to the city without her, but not daring to go back into the pass again. They had seen the creatures of the valley, and they were still afraid.

They gave mounts to the three. They themselves walked behind Ciara, and their heads were low with shame.

They came into Kushat through the riven gate, and Stark went with Ciara to the King City, where she made Balin follow too.

"Your sister is there," she said. "I have had her cared for."

The city was quiet, with the sullen apathy that follows after battle. The men of Mekh cheered Ciara in the streets. She rode proudly, but Stark saw that her face was gaunt and strained.

He, too, was marked deep by what he had seen and done, beyond the Gates of Death.

They went up into the castle.

Thanis took Balin into her arms, and wept. She had lost her first wild fury, and she could look at Ciara now with a restrained hatred that had a tinge almost of admiration.

"You fought for Kushat," she said, unwillingly, when she had heard the story. "For that, at least, I can thank you."

She went to Stark then, and looked up at him. "Kushat, and my brother's life. . . ." She kissed him, and there were tears on her lips. But she turned to Ciara with a bitter smile.

"No one can hold him, any more than the wind can be held. You will learn that."

She went out then with Balin, and left Stark and Ciara alone, in the chambers of the king.

Ciara said, "The little one is very shrewd." She unbuckled the hauberk and let it fall, standing slim in her tunic of black leather, and walked to the tall windows that looked out upon the mountains. She leaned her head wearily against the stone.

"An evil day, an evil deed. And now I have Kushat to govern, with no reward of power from beyond the Gates of Death. How man can be misled!"

Stark poured wine from the flagon and brought it to her. She looked at him over the rim of the cup, with a certain wry amusement.

"The little one is shrewd, and she is right. I don't know that I can be as wise as she. . . . Will you stay with me, Stark, or will you go?"

He did not answer at once, and she asked him, "What hunger drives you, Stark? It is not conquest, as it was with me. What are you looking for that you cannot find?"

He thought back across the years, back to the beginning—to the boy N'Chaka who had once been happy with Old One and little Tika, in the blaze and thunder and bitter frosts of a valley in the Twilight Belt of Mercury. He remembered how all that had ended, under the guns of the miners—the men who were his own kind.

He shook his head. "I don't know. It doesn't matter." He took her between his two hands, feeling the strength and the splendor of her, and it was oddly difficult to find words.

"I want to stay, Ciara. Now, this minute, I could promise that I would stay forever. But I know myself. You belong here, you will make Kushat your own. I don't. Someday I will go."

Ciara nodded. "My neck, also, was not made for chains, and one country was too little to hold me. Very well, Stark. Let it be so."

She smiled, and let the wine-cup fall.

A WORLD IS BORN

Mel Gray flung down his hoe with a sudden tigerish fierceness and stood erect. Tom Ward, working beside him, glanced at Gray's Indianesque profile, the youth of it hardened by war and the hells of the Eros prison blocks.

A quick flash of satisfaction crossed Ward's dark eyes. Then he grinned and said mockingly.

"Hell of a place to spend the rest of your life, ain't it?"

Mel Gray stared with slitted blue eyes down the valley. The huge sun of Mercury seared his naked body. Sweat channeled the dust on his skin. His throat ached with thirst. And the bitter landscape mocked him more than Wade's dark face.

"The rest of my life," he repeated softly. "The rest of my life!"

He was twenty-eight.

Wade spat in the damp black earth. "You ought to be glad—helping the unfortunate, building a haven for the derelict. . . ."

"Shut up!" Fury rose in Gray, hotter than the boiling springs that ran from the Sunside to water the valleys. He hated Mercury. He hated John Moulton and his daughter Jill, who had conceived this plan of building a new world for the destitute and desperate veterans of the Second Interplanetary War.

"I've had enough 'unselfish service'," he whispered. "I'm serving myself from now on."

Escape. That was all he wanted. Escape from these stifling valleys, from the snarl of the wind in the barren crags that towered higher than Everest into airless space. Escape from the surveillance of the twenty guards, the forced companionship of the ninety-nine other veteran-convicts.

Wade poked at the furrows between the sturdy hybrid tubers. "It ain't possible, kid. Not even for 'Duke' Gray, the 'light-fingered genius who held the Interstellar Police at a standstill for five years'." He laughed. "I read your publicity."

Gray stroked slow, earth-stained fingers over his sleek cap of yellow hair. "You think so?" he asked softly.

Dio the Martian came down the furrow, his lean, wiry figure silhouetted against the upper panorama of the valley; the neat rows of vegetables and the green riot of Venusian wheat, dotted with toiling men and their friendly guards.

Dio's green, narrowed eyes studied Gray's hard face.

"What's the matter, Gray? Trying to start something?"

"Suppose I were?" asked Gray silkily. Dio was the unofficial leader of the convict-veterans. There was about his thin body and hatchet face some of the grim determination that had made the Martians cling to their dying world and bring life to it again.

"You volunteered, like the rest of us," said the Martian. "Haven't you the guts to stick it?"

"The hell I volunteered! The IPA sent me. And what's it to you?"

"Only this." Dio's green eyes were slitted and ugly. "You've only been here a month. The rest of us came nearly a year ago—because we wanted to. We've worked like slaves, because we wanted to. In three weeks the crops will be in. The Moulton Project will be self-supporting. Moulton will get his permanent charter, and we'll be on our way.

"There are ninety-nine of us, Gray, who want the Moulton Project to succeed. We know that that louse Caron of Mars doesn't want it to, since pitchblende was discovered. We don't know whether you're working for him or not, but you're a troublemaker.

"There isn't to be any trouble, Gray. We're not giving the Interplanetary Prison Authority any excuse to revoke its decision and give Caron of Mars a free hand here. We'll see to anyone who tries it. Understand?"

Mel Gray took one slow step forward, but Ward's sharp, "Stow it! A guard," stopped him. The Martian worked back up the furrow. The guard, reassured, strolled back up the valley, squinting at the jagged streak of pale-grey sky that was going black as low clouds formed, only a few hundred feet above the copper cables that ran from cliff to cliff high over their heads.

"Another storm," growled Ward. "It gets worse as Mercury enters perihelion. Lovely world, ain't it?"

"Why did you volunteer?" asked Gray, picking up his hoe.

Ward shrugged. "I had my reasons."

Gray voiced the question that had troubled him since his transfer. "There were hundreds on the waiting list to replace the man who died. Why did they send me, instead?"

"Some fool blunder," said Ward carelessly. And then, in the same casual tone, "You mean it, about escaping?"

Gray stared at him. "What's it to you?"

Ward moved closer. "I can help you?"

A stab of mingled hope and wary suspicion transfixed Gray's heart. Ward's dark face grinned briefly into his, with a flash of secretive black eyes, and Gray was conscious of distrust.

"What do you mean, help me?"

Dio was working closer, watching them. The first growl of thunder rattled against the cliff faces. It was dark now, the pink flames of the Dark-side aurora visible beyond the valley mouth.

"I've got—connections," returned Ward cryptically. "Interested?"

Gray hesitated. There was too much he couldn't understand. Moreover, he was a lone wolf. Had been since the Second Interplanetary War wrenched him from the quiet backwater of his country home an eternity of eight years before and hammered him into hardness—a cynic who trusted nobody and nothing but Mel 'Duke' Gray.

"If you have connections," he said slowly, "why don't you use 'em yourself?"

"I got my reasons." Again that secretive grin. "But it's no hide off you, is it? All you want is to get away."

That was true. It would do no harm to hear what Ward had to say.

Lightning burst overhead, streaking down to be caught and grounded by the copper cables. The livid flare showed Dio's face, hard with worry and determination. Gray nodded.

"Tonight, then," whispered Ward. "In the barracks."

Out from the cleft where Mel Gray worked, across the flat plain of rock stripped naked by the wind that raved across it, lay the deep valley that sheltered the heart of the Moulton Project.

Hot springs joined to form a steaming river. Vegetation grew savagely under the huge sun. The air, kept at almost constant temperature by the blanketing effect of the hot springs, was stagnant and heavy.

But up above, high over the copper cables that crossed every valley where men ventured, the eternal wind of Mercury screamed and snarled between the naked cliffs.

Three concrete domes crouched on the valley floor, housing barracks, tool-shops, kitchens, store-houses, and executive quarters, connected by underground passages. Beside the smallest dome, joined to it by a heavily barred tunnel, was an insulated hangar, containing the only space ship on Mercury.

In the small dome, John Moulton leaned back from a pile of reports, took a pinch of Martian snuff, sneezed lustily, and said.

"Jill, I think we've done it."

The grey-eyed, black-haired young woman turned from the quartzite window through which she had been watching the gathering storm overhead. The thunder from other valleys reached them as a dim barrage which, at this time of Mercury's year, was never still.

"I don't know," she said. "It seems that nothing can happen now, and yet. . . . It's been too easy."

"Easy!" snorted Moulton. "We've broken our backs fighting these valleys. And our nerves, fighting time. But we've licked 'em!"

He rose, shaggy grey hair tousled, grey eyes alight.

"I told the IPA those men weren't criminals. And I was right. They can't deny me the charter now. No matter how much Caron of Mars would like to get his claws on this radium."

He took Jill by the shoulders and shook her, laughing.

"Three weeks, girl, that's all. First crops ready for harvest, first pay-ore coming out of the mines. In three weeks my permanent charter will have to be granted, according to agreement, and then. . . .

"Jill," he added solemnly, "we're seeing the birth of a world."

"That's what frightens me." Jill glanced upward as the first flare of lightning struck down, followed by a crash of thunder that shook the dome.

"So much can happen at a birth. I wish the three weeks were over!"

"Nonsense, girl! What could possibly happen?"

She looked at the copper cables, burning with the electricity running along them, and thought of the one hundred and twenty-two souls in that narrow Twilight Belt—with the fierce heat of the Sunside before them and the spatial cold of the Shadow side at their backs, fighting against wind and storm and heat to build a world to replace the ones the War had taken from them.

"So much could happen," she whispered. "An accident, an escape. . . ."

The inter-dome telescreen buzzed its signal. Jill, caught in a queer mood of premonition, went to it.

The face of Dio the Martian appeared on the screen, still wet and dirty from the storm-soaked fields, disheveled from his battle across the plain in the chaotic winds.

"I want to see you, Miss Moulton," he said. "There's something funny I think you ought to know."

"Of course," said Jill, and met her father's eyes. "I think we'll see, now, which one of us is right."

The barracks were quiet, except for the mutter of distant thunder and the heavy breathing of exhausted men. Tom Ward crouched in the darkness by Mel Gray's bunk.

"You ain't gonna go soft at the last minute, are you?" he whispered. "Because I can't afford to take chances."

"Don't worry," Gray returned grimly. "What's your proposition?"

"I can give you the combination to the lock of the hangar passage. All you have to do is get into Moulton's office, where the passage door is, and go to it. The ship's a two-seater. You can get her out of the valley easy."

Gray's eyes narrowed in the dark. "What's the catch?"

"There ain't none. I swear it."

"Look, Ward. I'm no fool. Who's behind this, and why?"

"That don't make no difference. All you want . . . ow!"

Gray's fingers had fastened like steel claws on his wrist.

"I get it, now," said Gray slowly. "That's why I was sent

here. Somebody wanted me to make trouble for Moulton." His fingers tightened agonizingly, and his voice sank to a slow drawl.

"I don't like being a pawn in somebody else's chess game."

"Okay, okay! It ain't my fault. Lemme go." Ward rubbed his bruised wrist. "Sure, somebody—I ain't sayin' who—sent you here, knowin' you'd want to escape. I'm here to help you. You get free, I get paid, the Big Boy gets what he wants. Okay?"

Gray was silent, scowling in the darkness. Then he said.

"All right. I'll take a chance."

"Then listen. You tell Moulton you have a complaint. I'll. . . ."

Light flooded the dark as the door clanged open. Ward leaped like a startled rabbit, but the light speared him, held him. Ward felt a pulse of excitement beat up in him.

The long ominous shadows of the guards raised elongated guns. The barracks stirred and muttered, like a vast aviary waking.

"Ward and Gray," said one of the guards. "Moulton wants you."

Gray rose from his bunk with the lithe, delicate grace of a cat. The monotony of sleep and labor was ended. Something had broken. Life was once again a moving thing.

John Moulton sat behind the untidy desk. Dio the Martian sat grimly against the wall. There was a guard beside him, watching.

Mel Gray noted all this as he and Ward came in. But his cynical blue eyes went beyond, to a door with a ponderous combination lock. Then they were attracted by something else—the tall, slim figure standing against the black quartz panes of the far wall.

It was the first time he had seen Jill Moulton. She looked the perfect sober apostle of righteousness he'd learned to mock. And then he saw the soft cluster of black curls, the curve of her throat above the dark dress, the red lips that balanced her determined jaw and direct grey eyes.

Moulton spoke, his shaggy head hunched between his shoulders.

"Dio tells me that you, Gray, are not a volunteer."

"Tattletale," said Gray. He was gauging the distance to the hangar door, the positions of the guards, the time it would take to spin out the combination. And he knew he couldn't do it.

"What were you and Ward up to when the guards came?"

"I couldn't sleep," said Gray amiably. "He was telling me bedtime stories." Jill Moulton was lovely, he couldn't deny that. Lovely, but not soft. She gave him an idea.

Moulton's jaw clamped. "Cut the comedy, Gray. Are you working for Caron of Mars?"

Caron of Mars, chairman of the board of the Interplanetary Prison Authority. Dio had mentioned him. Gray smiled in understanding. Caron of Mars had sent him, Gray, to Mercury. Caron of Mars was helping him, through Ward, to escape. Caron of Mars wanted Mercury for his own purposes—and he could have it.

"In a manner of speaking, Mr. Moulton," he said gravely, "Caron of Mars is working for me."

He caught Ward's sharp hiss of remonstrance. Then Jill Moulton stepped forward.

"Perhaps he doesn't understand what he's doing, Father." Her eyes met Gray's. "You want to escape, don't you?"

Gray studied her, grinning as the slow rose flushed her skin, the corners of her mouth tightening with anger.

"Go on," he said. "You have a nice voice."

Her eyes narrowed, but she held her temper.

"You must know what that would mean, Gray. There are thousands of veterans in the prisons now. Their offenses are mostly trivial, but the Prison Authority can't let them go, because they have no jobs, no homes, no money.

"The valleys here are fertile. There are mines rich in copper and pitchblende. The men have a chance for a home and a job, a part in building a new world. We hope to make Mercury an independent, self-governing member of the League of Worlds."

"With the Moultons as rulers, of course," Gray murmured.

"If they want us," answered Jill, deliberately missing the point. "Do you think you have the right to destroy all we've worked for?"

Gray was silent. Rather grimly, she went on.

"Caron of Mars would like to see us defeated. He didn't care about Mercury before radium was discovered. But now he'd like to turn it into a prison mining community, with convict labor, leasing mine grants to corporations and cleaning up big fortunes for himself and his associates.

"Any trouble here will give him an excuse to say that we've failed, that the Project is a menace to the Solar System. If you try to escape, you wreck everything we've done. If you don't tell the truth, you may cost thousands of men their futures.

"Do you understand? Will you cooperate?"

Gray said evenly, "I'm my own keeper, now. My brother will have to take care of himself."

It was ridiculously easy, she was so earnest, so close to him. He had a brief kaleidoscope of impressions—Ward's sullen bewilderment, Moulton's angry roar, Dio's jerky rise to his feet as the guards grabbed for their guns.

Then he had his hands around her slim, firm throat, her body pressed close to his, serving as a shield against bullets.

"Don't be rash," he told them all quietly. "I can break her neck quite easily, if I have to. Ward, unlock that door."

In utter silence, Ward darted over and began to spin the dial. At last he said, "Okay, c'mon."

Gray realized that he was sweating. Jill was like warm, rigid marble in his hands. And he had another idea.

"I'm going to take the girl as a hostage," he announced. "If I get safely away, she'll be turned loose, her health and virtue still intact. Good night."

The clang of the heavy door had a comforting sound behind them.

The ship was a commercial job, fairly slow but sturdy. Gray strapped Jill Moulton into one of the bucket seats in the control room and then checked the fuel and air gauges. The tanks were full.

"What about you?" he said to Ward. "You can't go back."

"Nah. I'll have to go with you. Warm her up, Duke, while I open the dome."

He darted out. Gray set the atmosphere motors idling. The dome slid open, showing the flicker of the auroras, where areas of intense heat and cold set up atmospheric tension by rapid fluctuation of adjoining air masses.

Mercury, cutting the vast magnetic field of the Sun in an eccentric orbit, tortured by the daily change from blistering heat to freezing cold in the thin atmosphere, was a powerful generator of electricity.

Ward didn't come back.

Swearing under his breath, tense for the sound of pursuit in spite of the girl, Gray went to look. Out beyond the hangar, he saw a figure running.

Running hard up into the narrowing cleft of the valley, where natural galleries in the rock of Mercury led to the places where the copper cables were anchored, and farther, into the unexplored mystery of the caves.

Gray scowled, his arrogant Roman profile hard against the flickering aurora. Then he slammed the lock shut.

The ship roared out into the tearing winds of the plain. Gray cut in his rockets and blasted up, into the airless dark among the high peaks.

Jill Moulton hadn't moved or spoken.

Gray snapped on the space radio, leaving his own screen dark. Presently he picked up signals in a code he didn't know.

"Listen," he said. "I knew there was some reason for Ward's running out on me."

His Indianesque face hardened. "So that's the game! They want to make trouble for you by letting me escape and then make themselves heroes by bringing me in, preferably dead.

"They've got ships waiting to get me as soon as I clear Mercury, and they're getting stand-by instructions from somebody on the ground. The somebody that Ward was making for."

Jill's breath made a small hiss. "Somebody's near the Project. . . ."

Gray snapped on his transmitter.

"Duke Gray, calling all ships off Mercury. Will the flagship of your reception committee please come in?"

His screen flickered to life. A man's face appeared—the middle-aged, soft-fleshed, almost stickily innocent face of one of the Solar Systems greatest crusaders against vice and crime.

Jill Moulton gasped. "Caron of Mars!"

"Ward gave the game away," said Gray gently. "Too bad."

The face of Caron of Mars never changed expression. But behind those flesh-hooded eyes was a cunning brain, working at top speed.

"I have a passenger," Gray went on. "Miss Jill Moulton. I'm responsible for her safety, and I'd hate to have her inconvenienced."

The tip of a pale tongue flicked across Caron's pale lips.

"That is a pity," he said, with the intonation of a preaching minister. "But I cannot stop the machinery set in motion. . . ."

"And besides," finished Gray acidly, "you think that if Jill Moulton dies with me, it'll break John Moulton so he won't fight you at all."

His lean hand poised on the switch.

"All right, you putrid flesh-tub. Try and catch us!"

The screen went dead. Gray hunched over the controls. If he could get past them, lose himself in the glare of the Sun. . . .

He looked aside at the stony-faced girl beside him. She was studying him contemptuously out of hard gray eyes.

"How," she said slowly, "can you be such a callous swine?"

"Callous?" He controlled the quite unreasonable anger that rose in him. "Not at all. The war taught me that if I didn't look out for myself, no one would."

"And yet you must have started out a human being."

He laughed.

The ship burst into searing sunlight. The Sunside of Mercury blazed below them. Out toward the velvet dark of space the side of a waiting ship flashed burning silver.

Even as he watched, the flare of its rockets arced against the blackness. They had been sighted.

Gray's practised eye gauged the stranger's speed against his own, and he cursed softly. Abruptly he wheeled the ship and started down again, cutting his rockets as the shadow swallowed them.

The ship was eerily silent, dropping with a rising scream as the atmosphere touched the hull.

"What are you going to do?" asked Jill almost too quietly.

He didn't answer. Maneuvering the ship on velocity between those stupendous pinnacles took all his attention. Caron, at least, couldn't follow him in the dark without exhaust flares as guides.

They swept across the wind-torn plain, into the mouth of the valley where Gray had worked, braking hard to a stop under the cables.

"You might have got past them," said Jill.

"One chance in a hundred."

Her mouth twisted. "Afraid to take it?"

He smiled harshly. "I haven't yet reached the stage where I kill women. You'll be safe here—the men will find you in the morning. I'm going back, alone."

"Safe!" she said bitterly. "For what? No matter what happens, the Project is ruined."

"Don't worry," he told her brutally. "You'll find some other way to make a living."

Her eyes blazed. "You think that's all its means to us? Just money and power?" She whispered, "I hope they kill you, Duke Gray!"

He rose lazily and opened the air lock, then turned and freed her. And, sharply, the valley was bathed in a burst of light.

"Damn!" Gray picked up the sound of air motors overhead. "They must have had infra-red search beams. Well, that does it. We'll have to run for it, since this bus isn't armed."

With eerie irrelevancy, the teleradio buzzed. At this time of night, after the evening storms, some communication was possible.

Gray had a hunch. He opened the switch, and the face of John Moulton appeared on the screen. It was white and oddly still.

"Our guards saw your ship cross the plain," said Moulton quietly. "The men of the Project, led by Dio, are coming for you. I sent them, because I have decided that the life of my daughter is less important than the lives of many thousands of people.

"I appeal to you, Gray, to let her go. Her life won't save you.

And it's very precious to me."

Caron's ship swept over, low above the cables, and the grinding concussion of a bomb lifted the ship, hurled it down with the stern end twisted to uselessness. The screen went dead.

Gray caught the half stunned girl. "I wish to heaven I could get rid of you!" he grated. "And I don't know why I don't!"

But she was with him when he set out down the valley, making for the cliff caves, up where the copper cables were anchored.

Caron's ship, a fast, small fighter, wheeled between the cliffs and turned back. Gray dropped flat, holding the girl down. Bombs pelted them with dirt and uprooted vegetables, started fires in the wheat. The pilot found a big enough break in the cables and came in for a landing.

Gray was up and running again. He knew the way into the explored galleries. From there on, it was anybody's guess.

Caron was brazen enough about it. The subtle way had failed. Now he was going all out. And he was really quite safe. With the broken cables to act as conductors, the first thunderstorm would obliterate all proof of his activities in this valley. Mercury, because of its high electrical potential, was cut off from communication with other worlds. Moulton, even if he had knowledge of what went on, could not send for help.

Gray wondered briefly what Caron intended to do in case he, Gray, made good his escape. That outpost in the main valley, for which Ward had been heading, wasn't kept for fun. Besides, Caron was too smart to have only one string to his bow.

Shouts, the spatter of shots around them. The narrow trail loomed above. Gray sent the girl scrambling up.

The sun burst up over the high peaks, leaving the black shadow of the valley still untouched. Caron's ship roared off. But six of its crew came after Gray and Jill Moulton.

The chill dark of the tunnel mouth swallowed them. Keeping right to avoid the great copper posts that held the cables, strung through holes drilled in the solid rock of the gallery's outer wall, Gray urged the girl along.

The cleft his hand was searching for opened. Drawing the girl inside, around a jutting shoulder, he stopped, listening.

Footsteps echoed outside, grew louder, swept by. There was no light. But the steps were too sure to have been made in the dark.

"Infra-red torches and goggles," Gray said tersely, "You see, but your quarry doesn't. Useful gadget. Come on."

"But where? What are you going to do?"

"Escape, girl. Remember? They smashed my ship. But there must be another one on Mercury. I'm going to find it."

"I don't understand."

"You probably never will. Here's where I leave you. That Martian Galahad will be along any minute. He'll take you home."

Her voice came soft and puzzled through the dark.

"I don't understand you, Gray. You wouldn't risk my life. Yet you're turning me loose, knowing that I might save you, knowing that I'll hunt you down if I can. I thought you were a hardened cynic."

"What makes you think I'm not?"

"If you were, you'd have kicked me out the waste tubs of the ship and gone on. You'd never have turned back."

"I told you," he said roughly, "I don't kill women." He turned away, but her harsh chuckle followed him.

"You're a fool, Gray. You've lost truth—and you aren't even true to your lie."

He paused, in swift anger. Voices the sound of running men, came up from the path. He broke into a silent run, following the dying echoes of Caron's men.

"Run, Gray!" cried Jill. "Because we're coming after you!"

The tunnels, ancient blowholes for the volcanic gases that had tortured Mercury with the raising of the titanic mountains, sprawled in a labyrinthine network through those same vast peaks. Only the galleries lying next the valleys had been explored. Man's habitation on Mercury had been too short.

Gray could hear Caron's men circling about through connecting tunnels, searching. It proved what he had already guessed. He was taking a desperate chance. But the way back was closed—and he was used to taking chances.

The geography of the district was clear in his mind—the valley he had just left and the main valley, forming an obtuse angle with the apex out on the wind-torn plain and a double range of mountains lying out between the sides of the triangle.

Somewhere there was a passage through those peaks. Somewhere there was a landing place, and ten to one there was a ship on it. Caron would never have left his men stranded, on the off chance that they might be discovered and used in evidence against him.

The men now hunting him knew their way through the tunnels, probably with the aid of markings that fluoresced under infra-red light. They were going to take him through, too.

They were coming closer. He waited far up in the main gallery, in the mouth of a side tunnel. Now, behind them, he could hear Dio's men. The noise of Caron's outfit stopped, then began again, softly.

Gray smiled, his sense of humor pleased. He tensed, waiting.

The rustle of cloth, the furtive creak of leather, the clink of metal equipment. Heavy breathing. Somebody whispered,

"Who the hell's that back there?"

"Must be men from the Project. We'd better hurry."

"We've got to find that damned Gray first," snapped the first voice grimly. "Caron'll burn us if we don't."

Gray counted six separate footsteps, trying to allow for the echoes. When he was sure the last man was by, he stepped out. The noise of Dio's hunt was growing—there must be a good many of them.

Covered by their own echoes, he stole up on the men ahead. His groping hand brushed gently against the clothing of the last man in the group. Gauging his distance swiftly, he went into action.

One hand fastened over the fellow's mouth. The other, holding a good-sized rock, struck down behind the ear. Gray eased the body down with scarcely a sound.

Their uniforms, he had noticed, were not too different from his prison garb. In a second he had stripped goggles, cap, and gun-belt from the body, and was striding after the others.

They moved like five eerie shadows now, in the queer light of the leader's lamp. Small fluorescent markings guided them. The last man grunted over his shoulder,

"What happened to you?"

"Stumbled," whispered Gray tersely, keeping his head down. A whisper is a good disguise for the voice. The other nodded.

"Don't straggle. No fun, getting lost in here."

The leader broke in. "We'll circle again. Be careful of that Project bunch—they'll be using ordinary light. And be quiet!"

They went, through connecting passages. The noise of Dio's party grew ominously loud. Abruptly, the leader swore.

"Caron or no Caron, he's gone. And we'd better go, too."

He turned off, down a different tunnel, and Gray heaved a sigh of relief, remembering the body he'd left in the open. For a time the noise of their pursuers grew remote. And then, suddenly, there was an echoing clamor of footsteps, and the glare of torches on the wall of a cross-passage ahead.

Voices came to Gray, distorted by the rock vaults.

"I'm sure I heard them, just then." It was Jill's voice.

"Yeah." That was Dio. "The trouble is, where?"

The footsteps halted. Then, "Let's try this passage. We don't want to get too far into this maze."

Caron's leader blasphemed softly and dodged into a side tunnel. The man next to Gray stumbled and cried out with pain as he struck the wall, and a shout rose behind them.

The leader broke into a run, twisting, turning, diving into the maze of smaller tunnels. The sounds of pursuit faded, were lost in the tomblike silence of the caves. One of the men laughed.

"We sure lost 'em!"

"Yeah," said the leader. "We lost 'em, all right." Gray caught the note of panic in his voice. "We lost the markers, too."

"You mean . . . ?"

"Yeah. Turning off like that did it. Unless we can find that marked tunnel, we're sunk!"

Gray, silent in the shadows, laughed a bitter, ironic laugh.

* * * *

They went on, stumbling down endless black halls, losing all track of branching corridors, straining to catch the first glint of saving light. Once or twice they caught the echoes of Dio's party, and knew that they, too, were lost and wandering.

Then, quite suddenly, they came out into a vast gallery, running like a subway tube straight to left and right. A wind tore down it, hot as a draught from the burning gates of Hell.

It was a moment before anyone grasped the significance of that wind. Then someone shouted,

"We're saved! All we have to do is walk against it!"

They turned left, almost running in the teeth of that searing blast. And Gray began to notice a peculiar thing.

The air was charged with electricity. His clothing stiffened and crackled. His hair crawled on his head. He could see the faint discharges of sparks from his companions.

Whether it was the effect of the charged air, or the reaction from the nervous strain of the past hours, Mel Gray began to be afraid.

Weary to exhaustion, they struggled on against the burning wind. And then they blundered out into a cave, huge as a cathedral, lighted by a queer, uncertain bluish light.

Gray caught the sharp smell of ozone. His whole body was tingling with electric tension. The bluish light seemed to be in indeterminate lumps scattered over the rocky floor. The rush of the wind under that tremendous vault was terrifying.

They stopped, Gray keeping to the background. Now was the time to evade his unconscious helpers. The moment they reached daylight, he'd be discovered.

Soft-footed as a cat, he was already hidden among the heavy shadows of the fluted walls when he heard voices from off to the right, a confused shout of men under fearful strain, growing louder and louder, underscored with the tramp of footsteps. Lights blazed suddenly in the cathedral dark, and from the mouth of a great tunnel some hundred yards away, the men of the Project poured into the cave.

And then, sharp and high and unexpected, a man screamed.

* * * *

The lumps of blue light were moving. And a man had died. He lay on the rock, his flesh blackened jelly, with a rope of glowing light running from the metal of his gun butt to the metal buttons on his cap.

All across the vast floor of that cavern the slow, eerie ripple of motion grew. The scattered lumps melted and flowed together, converging in wavelets of blue flame upon the men.

The answer came to Gray. Those things were some form of energy-life, born of the tremendous electric tensions on Mercury. Like all electricity, they were attracted to metal.

In a sudden frenzy of motion, he ripped off his metal-framed goggles, his cap and gun-belt. The Moultons forbade metal because of the danger of lightning, and his boots were made of rubber, so he felt reasonably safe, but a tense fear ran in prickling waves across his skin.

Guns began to bark, their feeble thunder all but drowned in the vast rush of the wind. Bullets struck the oncoming waves of light with no more effect than the eruption of a shower of sparks. Gray's attention, somehow, was riveted on Jill, standing with Dio at the head of her men.

She wore ordinary light slippers, having been dressed only for indoors. And there were silver ornaments at waist and throat.

He might have escaped, then, quite unnoticed. Instead, for a reason even he couldn't understand, he ran for Jill Moulton.

The first ripples of blue fire touched the ranks of Dio's men. Bolts of it leaped upward to fasten upon gun-butts and the buckles of the cartridge belts. Men screamed, fell, and died.

An arm of the fire licked out, driving in behind Dio and the girl. The guns of Caron's four remaining men were silent, now.

Gray leaped over that hissing electric surf, running toward Jill. A hungry worm of light reared up, searching for Dio's gun. Gray's hand swept it down, to be instantly buried in a mass of glowing ropes. Dio's hatchet face snarled at him in startled anger.

Jill cried out as Gray tore the silver ornaments from her dress. "Throw down the guns!" he yelled. "It's metal they want!"

He heard his name shouted by men torn momentarily from their own terror. Dio cried, "Shoot him!" A few bullets whined past, but their immediate fear spoiled both aim and attention.

Gray caught up Jill and began to run, toward the tube from which the wind howled in the cave. Behind him, grimly, Dio followed.

The electric beasts didn't notice him. His insulated feet trampled through them, buried to the ankle in living flame, feeling queer tenuous bodies break and reform.

The wind met them like a physical barrier at the tunnel mouth. Gray put Jill down. The wind strangled him. He tore off his coat and wrapped it over the girl's head, using his shirt over his own. Jill, her black curls whipped straight, tried to fight back past him, and he saw Dio coming, bent double against the wind.

He saw something else. Something that made him grab Jill and point, his flesh crawling with swift, cold dread.

The electric beasts had finished their pleasure. The dead were cinders on the rock. The living had run back into the tunnels. And now the blue sea of fire was flowing again, straight toward the place where they stood.

It was flowing fast, and Gray sensed an urgency, an impersonal haste, as though a command had been laid upon those living ropes of flame.

The first dim rumble of thunder rolled down the wind. Gripping Jill, Gray turned up the tunnel.

The wind, compressed in that narrow throat of rock, beat them blind and breathless, beat them to their bellies, to crawl. How long it took them, they never knew.

But Gray caught glimpses of Dio the Martian crawling behind them, and behind him again, the relentless flow of the fire-things.

They floundered out onto a rocky slope, fell away beneath the suck of the wind, and lay still, gasping. It was hot. Thunder crashed abruptly, and lightning flared between the cliffs.

Gray felt a contracting of the heart. There were no cables.

Then he saw it—the small, fast fighter flying below them on a flat plateau. A cave mouth beside it had been closed with a plastic door. The ship was the one that had followed them. He guessed at another one behind the protecting door.

Raking the tumbled blond hair out of his eyes, Gray got up.

Jill was still sitting, her black curls bowed between her hands. There wasn't much time, but Gray yielded to impulse. Pulling her head back by the silken hair, he kissed her.

"If you ever get tired of virtue, sweetheart, look me up." But somehow he wasn't grinning, and he ran down the slope.

He was almost to the open lock of the ship when things began to happen. Dio staggered out of the wind-tunnel and sagged down beside Jill. Then, abruptly, the big door opened.

Five men came out—one in pilot's costume, two in nondescript apparel, one in expensive business clothes, and the fifth in dark prison garb.

Gray recognized the last two. Caron of Mars and the errant Ward.

They were evidently on the verge of leaving. But they looked cheerful. Caron's sickly-sweet face all but oozed honey, and Ward was grinning his rat's grin.

Thunder banged and rolled among the rocks. Lightning flared in the cloudy murk. Gray saw the hull of a second ship beyond the door. Then the newcomers had seen him, and the two on the slope.

Guns ripped out of holsters. Gray's heart began to pound slowly. He, and Jill and Dio, were caught on that naked slope, with the flood of electric death at their backs.

His Indianesque face hardened. Bullets whined round him as he turned back up the slope, but he ran doubled over, putting all his hope in the tricky, uncertain light.

Jill and the Martian crouched stiffly, not knowing where to turn. A flare of lightning showed Gray the first of the firethings, flowing out onto the ledge, hidden from the men below.

"Back into the cave!" he yelled. His urgent hand fairly lifted Dio. The Martian glared at him, then obeyed. Bullets snarled against the rock. The light was too bad for accurate shooting, but luck couldn't stay with them forever.

Gray glanced over his shoulder as they scrambled up on the

ledge. Caron waited by his ship. Ward and the others were charging the slope. Gray's teeth gleamed in a cruel grin.

Sweeping Jill into his arms, he stepped into the lapping flow of fire. Dio swore viciously, but he followed. They started toward the cave mouth, staggering in the rush of the wind.

"For God's sake, don't fall," snapped Gray. "Here they come!"

The pilot and one of the nondescript men were the first over. They were into the river of fire before they knew, it, and then it was too late. One collapsed and was buried. The pilot fell backward, and then other man died under his body, of a broken neck.

Ward stopped. Gray could see his face, dark and hard and calculating. He studied Gray and Dio, and the dead men. He turned and looked back at Caron. Then, deliberately, he stripped off his gun belt, threw down his gun, and waded into the river.

Gray remembered, then, that Ward too wore rubber boots, and had no metal on him.

Ward came on, the glowing ropes sliding surf-like around his boots. Very carefully. Gray handed Jill to Dio.

"If I die too," he said, "there's only Caron down there. He's too fat to stop you."

Jill spoke, but he turned his back. He was suddenly confused, and it was almost pleasant to be able to lose his confusion in fighting. Ward had stopped some five feet away. Now he untied the length of tough cord that served him for a belt.

Gray nodded. Ward would try to throw a twist around his ankle and trip him. Once his body touched those swarming creatures. . . .

He tensed, watchfully. The rat's grin was set on Ward's dark face. The cord licked out.

But it caught Gray's throat instead of his ankle!

Ward laughed and braced himself. Cursing, Gray caught at the rope. But friction held it, and Ward pulled, hard. His face purpling, Gray could still commend Ward's strategy. In taking Gray off guard, he'd more than made up what he lost in point of leverage.

Letting his body go with the pull, Gray flung himself at Ward.

Blood blinded him, his heart was pounding, but he thought he foresaw Ward's next move. He let himself be pulled almost within striking distance.

Then, as Ward stepped, aside, jerking the rope and thrusting out a tripping foot, Gray made a catlike shift of balance and bent over.

His hands almost touched that weird, flowing surf as they clasped Ward's boot. Throwing all his strength into the lift, he hurled Ward backward.

Ward screamed once and disappeared under the blue fire. Gray clawed the rope from his neck. And then, suddenly, the world began to sway under him. He knew he was falling.

Some one's hand caught him, held him up. Fighting down his vertigo as his breath came back, he saw that it was Jill.

"Why?" he gasped, but her answer was lost in a titanic roar of thunder. Lightning blasted down. Dio's voice reached him, thin and distant through the clamor.

"We'll be killed! These damn things will attract the bolts!"

It was true. All his work had been for nothing. Looking up into that low, angry sky, Gray knew he was going to die.

Quite irrelevantly, Jill's words in the tunnel came back to him. "You're a fool . . . lost truth . . . not true to lie!"

Now, in this moment, she couldn't lie to him. He caught her shoulders cruelly, trying to read her eyes.

Very faintly through the uproar, he heard her. "I'm sorry for you, Gray. Good man, gone to waste."

Dio stifled a scream. Thunder crashed between the sounding boards of the cliffs. Gray looked up.

A titanic bolt of lightning shot down, straight for them. The burning blue surf was agitated, sending up pseudopods uncannily like worshipping arms. The bolt struck.

The air reeked of ozone, but Gray felt no shock. There was a hiss, a vast stirring of creatures around him. The blue light glowed, purpled.

Another bolt struck down, and another, and still they were not dead. The fire-things had become a writhing, joyous tangle of tenuous bodies, glowing bright and brighter.

Stunned, incredulous, the three humans stood. The light was now an eye-searing violet. Static electricity tingled through them in eerie waves. But they were not burned.

"My God," whispered Gray. "They eat it. They eat lightning!"

Not daring to move, they stood watching that miracle of alien life, the feeding of living things on raw current. And when the last bolt had struck, the tide turned and rolled back down the wind-tunnel, a blinding river of living light.

Silently, the three humans went down the rocky slope to where Caron of Mars cowered in the silver ship. No bolt had come near it. And now Caron came to meet them.

His face was pasty with fear, but the old cunning still lurked in his eyes.

"Gray," he said. "I have an offer to make."

"Well?"

"You killed my pilot," said Caron suavely. "I can't fly, myself. Take me off, and I'll pay you anything you want."

"In bullets," retorted Gray. "You won't want witnesses to this."

"Circumstances force me. Physically, you have the advantage."

Jill's fingers caught his arm. "Don't, Gray! The Project. . . ."

Caron faced her. "The Project is doomed in any case. My men carried out my secondary instructions. All the cables in your valley have been cut. There is a storm now ready to break.

"In fifteen minutes or so, everything will be destroyed, except the domes. Regrettable, but. . . ." He shrugged.

Jill's temper blazed, choking her so that she could hardly speak.

"Look at him, Gray," she whispered. "That's what you're so proud of being. A cynic, who believes in nothing but himself. Look at him!"

Gray turned on her.

"Damn you!" he grated. "Do you expect me to believe you, with the world full of hypocrites like him?"

Her eyes stopped him. He remembered Moulton, pleading for her life. He remembered how she had looked back there at the tunnel, when they had been sure of death. Some of his assurance was shaken.

"Listen," he said harshly. "I can save your valley. There's a chance in a million of coming out alive. Will you die for what you believe in?"

She hesitated, just for a second. Then she looked at Dio and said, "Yes."

Gray turned. Almost lazily, his fist snapped up and took Caron on his flabby jaw.

"Take care of him, Dio," he grunted. Then he entered the ship, herding the white-faced girl before him.

The ship hurtled up into airless space, where the blinding sunlight lay in sharp shadows on the rock. Over the ridge and down again, with the Project hidden under a surf of storm-clouds.

Cutting in the air motors, Gray dropped. Black, bellowing darkness swallowed them. Then he saw the valley, with the copper cables fallen, and the wheat already on fire in several places.

Flying with every bit of his skill, he sought the narrowest part of the valley and flipped over in a racking loop. The stern tubes hit rock. The nose slammed down on the opposite wall, wedging the ship by sheer weight.

Lightning gathered in a vast javelin and flamed down upon them. Jill flinched and caught her breath. The flame hissed along the hull and vanished into seared and blackened rock.

"Still willing to die for principle?" asked Gray brutally.

She glared at him. "Yes," she snapped. "But I hate having to die in your company!"

She looked down at the valley. Lightning struck with monotonous regularity on the hull, but the valley was untouched. Jill smiled, though her face was white, her body rigid with waiting.

It was the smile that did it. Gray looked at her, her tousled black curls, the lithe young curves of throat and breast. He leaned back in his seat, scowling out at the storm.

"Relax," he said. "You aren't going to die."

She turned on him, not daring to speak. He went on, slowly.

"The only chance you took was in the landing. We're acting as lightning rod for the whole valley, being the highest and best conductor. But, as a man named Faraday proved, the charge resides on the surface of the conductor. We're perfectly safe."

"How dared you!" she whispered.

He faced her, almost angrily.

"You knocked the props out from under my philosophy. I've had enough hypocritical eyewash. I had to prove you. Well, I have."

She was quiet for some time. Then she said, "I understand, Duke. I'm glad. And now what, for you?"

He shrugged wryly.

"I don't know. I can still take Caron's other ship and escape. But I don't think I want to. I think perhaps I'll stick around and give virtue another whirl."

Smoothing back his sleek fair hair, he shot her a sparkling look from under his hands.

"I won't," he added softly, "even mind going to Sunday School, if you were the teacher."

CHILD OF THE SUN

Eric Falken stood utterly still, staring down at his leashed and helpless hands on the controls of the spaceship Falcon.

The red lights on his indicator panel showed Hiltonist ships in a three-dimensional half-moon, above, behind, and below him. Pincer jaws, closing fast.

The animal instinct of escape prodded him, but he couldn't obey. He had fuel enough for one last burst of speed. But there was no way through that ring of ships. Tractor-beams, crisscrossing between them, would net the Falcon like a fish.

There was no way out ahead, either. Mercury was there, harsh and bitter in the naked blaze of the sun. The ships of Gantry Hilton, President of the Federation of Worlds, inventor of the Psycho-Adjuster, and ruler of men's souls, were herding him down to a landing at the lonely Spaceguard outpost.

A landing he couldn't dodge. And then . . .

For Paul Avery, a choice of death or Happiness. For himself and Sheila Moore, there was no choice. It was death.

The red lights blurred before Falken's eyes. The throb of the plates under his feet faded into distance. He'd stood at the controls for four chronometer days, ever since the Hiltonists had chased him up from Losangles, back on Earth.

He knew it was because he was exhausted that he couldn't think, or stop the nightmare of the past days from tramping through his brain, hammering the incessant question at him. How?

How had the Hiltonists traced him back from New York? Paul Avery, the Unregenerate recruit he went to get, had passed a rigid psycho-search—which, incidentally, revealed the finest brain ever to come to the Unregenerate cause. He couldn't be a spy. And he'd spoken to no one but Falken.

Yet they were traced. Hiltonist Black Guards were busy now, destroying the last avenues of escape from Earth, avenues that he, Falken, had led them through.

But how? He knew he hadn't given himself away. For thirty years he'd been spiriting Unregenerates away from Gantry Hilton's strongholds of Peace and Happiness. He was too old a hand for blunders.

Yet, somehow, the Black Guards caught up with them at Losangles, where the Falcon lay hidden. And, somehow, they got away, with a starving green-eyed girl named Kitty. . . .

"Not Kitty," Falken muttered. "Kitty's Happy. Hilton took Kitty, thirty years ago. On our wedding day."

A starving waif named Sheila Moore, who begged him for help, because he was Eric Falken and almost a god to the Unregenerates. They got away in the Falcon, but the Hiltonist ships followed.

Driven, hopeless flight, desperate effort to shake pursuit before he was too close to the Sun. Time and again, using precious fuel and accelerations that tried even his tough body, Falken thought he had escaped.

But they found him again. It was uncanny, the way they found him.

Now he couldn't run any more. At least he'd led the Hiltonists away from the pitiful starving holes where his people hid, on the outer planets and barren asteroids and dark derelict hulks floating far outside the traveled lanes.

And he'd kill himself before the Hiltonist psycho-search could pick his brain of information about the Unregenerates. Kill himself, if he could wake up.

He began to laugh, a drunken, ragged chuckle. He couldn't stop laughing. He clung to the panel edge and laughed until the tears ran down his scarred, dark face.

"Stop it," said Sheila Moore. "Stop it, Falken!"

"Can't. It's funny. We live in hell for thirty years, we Unregenerates, fighting Hiltonism. We're licked, now. We were before we started. Now I'm going to die so they can suffer hell a few weeks more. It's so damned funny!"

Sleep dragged at him. Sleep, urgent and powerful. So powerful that it seemed like an outside force gripping his mind. His hands relaxed on the panel edge.

"Falken," said Sheila Moore. "Eric Falken!"

Some steely thing in her voice lashed him erect again. She crouched on the shelf bunk against the wall, her feral green eyes blazing, her thin body taut in its torn green silk.

"You've got to get away, Falken. You've got to escape."

He had stopped laughing.

"Why?" he asked dully.

"We need you, Falken. You're a legend, a hope we cling to. If you give up, what are we to go on?"

She rose and paced the narrow deck. Paul Avery watched her from the bunk on the opposite wall, his amber eyes dull with the deep weariness that slackened his broad young body.

Falken watched her, too. The terrible urge for sleep hammered at him, bowed his grey-shot, savage head, drew the strength from his lean muscles. But he watched Sheila Moore.

That was why he had risked his life, and Avery's, and broken Unregenerate law to save her, unknown and untested. She blazed, somehow. She stabbed his brain with the same cold fire he had felt after Kitty was taken from him.

"You've got to escape," she said. "We can't give up yet."

Her voice was distant, her raw-gold hair a detached haze of light. Darkness crept on Falken's brain.

"How?" he whispered.

"I don't know . . . Falken!" She caught him with thin painful fingers. "They're driving you down on Mercury. Why not trick them? Why not go—beyond?"

He stared at her. Even he would never have thought of that. Beyond the orbit of Mercury there was only death.

Avery leaped to his feet. For a startled instant Falken's brain cleared, and he saw the trapped, wild terror in Avery's face.

"We'd die," said Avery hoarsely. "The heat . . ."

Sheila faced him. "We'll die anyway, unless you want Psycho-Change. Why not try it, Eric? Their instruments won't work close to the Sun. They may even be afraid to follow." The wiry, febrile force of her beat at them. "Try, Eric. We have nothing to lose."

Paul Avery stared from one to the other of them and then to the red lights that were ships. Abruptly he sank down on the edge of his bunk and dropped his broad, fair head in his hands. Falken saw the cords like drawn harp-strings on the backs of them.

"I . . . can't," whispered Falken. The command to sleep was once more a vast shout in his brain. "I can't think."

"You must!" said Sheila. "If you sleep, we'll be taken. You won't be able to kill yourself. They'll pick your brain empty. Then they'll Hiltonize you with the Psycho-Adjuster. They'll blank your brain with electric impulses and then transmit a whole new memory-pattern, even shifting the thought-circuits so that you won't think the same way. They'll change your metabolism, your glandular balance, your pigmentation, your face, and your finger-prints."

He knew she was recounting these things deliberately, to force him to fight. But still the weak darkness shrouded him.

"Even your name will be gone," she said. "You'll be placid and lifeless, lazing your life away, just one of Hilton's cattle." She took a deep breath and added, "Like Kitty."

He caught her shoulders, then, grinding the thin bone of them. "How did you know?"

"That night, when you saw me, you said her name. Perhaps I made you think of her. I know how it feels, Eric. They took the boy I loved away from me."

He clung to her, the blue distant fire in his eyes taking life from the hot, green blaze of hers. There was iron in her. He could feel the spark and clash of it against his mind.

"Talk to me," he whispered. "Keep me awake. I'll try."

Waves of sleep clutched Falken with physical hands. But he turned to the control panel.

The bitter blaze of Mercury stabbed his bloodshot eyes. Red lights hemmed him in. He couldn't think. And then Sheila Moore began to talk. Standing behind him, her thin vital hands on his shoulders, telling him the story of Hiltonism.

"Gantry Hilton's Psycho-Adjuster was a good thing at first. Through the mapping and artificial blanking of brain-waves and the use of electro-hypnotism—the transmission of thought-pat-terns directly to the brain—it cured non-lesional insanity, neuro-ses, and criminal tendencies. Then, at the end of the Interplanetary War . . ."

Red lights closing in. How could he get past the Spaceguard

battery? Sheila's voice fought back the darkness. Speed, that was what he needed. And more guts than he'd ever had to use in his life before. And luck.

"Keep talking, Sheila. Keep me awake."

". . . Hilton boomed his discovery. The people were worn out with six years of struggle. They wanted Hiltonism, Peace and Happiness. The passion for escape from life drove them like lunatics."

He found the emergency lever and thrust it down. The last ounce of hoarded power slammed into the rocket tubes. The Falcon reared and staggered.

Then she shot straight for Mercury, with the thin high scream of tortured metal shivering along the cabin walls.

Spaceshells burst. They shook the Falcon, but they were far behind. The ring of red lights was falling away. Acceleration tore at Falken's body, but the web of sleep was loosening. Sheila's voice cried to him, the story of man's slavery.

The naked, hungry peaks of Mercury snarled at Falken. And then the guns of the Spaceguard post woke up.

"Talk, Sheila!" he cried. "Keep talking!"

"So Gantry Hilton made himself a sort of God, regulating the thoughts and emotions of his people. There is no opposition now, except for the Unregenerates, and we have no power. Humanity walks in a placid stupor. It cannot feel dissatisfaction, disloyalty, or the will to grow and change. It cannot fight, even morally.

"Gantry Hilton is a god. His son after him will be a god. And humanity is dying."

There was a strange, almost audible snap in Falken's brain. He felt a quick, terrible stab of hate that startled him because it seemed no part of himself. Then it was gone, and his mind was clear.

He was tired to exhaustion, but he could think, and fight.

Livid, flaming stars leaped and died around him. Racked plates screamed in agony. Falken's lean hands raced across the controls. He knew now what he was going to do.

Down, down, straight into the black, belching mouths of the guns, gambling that his sudden burst of speed would confuse the gunners, that the tiny speck of his ship hurtling bow-on would be hard to see against the star-flecked depths of space.

Falken's lips were white. Sheila's thin hands were a sharp unnoticed pain on his shoulders. Down, down. . . . The peaks of Mercury almost grazed his hull.

A shell burst searingly, dead ahead. Blinded, dazed, Falken held his ship by sheer instinct. Thundering rockets fought the gravitational pull for a moment. Then he was through, and across.

Across Mercury, in free space, a speeding mote lost against the titanic fires of the Sun.

Falken turned. Paul Avery lay still in his bunk, but his golden eyes were wide, staring at Falken. They dropped to Sheila Moore, who had slipped exhausted to the floor, and came back to Falken and stared and stared with a queer, stark look that Falken couldn't read.

Falken cut the rockets and locked the controls. Heat was already seeping through the hull. He looked through shaded ports at the vast and swollen Sun.

No man in the history of space travel had ventured so close before. He wondered how long they could stand the heat, and whether the hull could screen off the powerful radiations.

His brain, with all its knowledge of the Unregenerate camps, was safe for a time. Knowing the hopelessness of it, he smiled sardonically, wondering if sheer habit had taken the place of reason.

Then Sheila's bright head made him think of Kitty, and he knew that his tired body had betrayed him. He could never give up.

He went down beside Sheila. He took her hands and said:

"Thank you. Thank you, Sheila Moore."

And then, quite peacefully, he was asleep with his head in her lap.

The heat was a malignant, vampire presence. Eric Falken felt it even before he wakened. He was lying in Avery's bunk, and the sweat that ran from his body made a sticky pool under him.

Sheila lay across from him, eyes closed, raw-gold hair pushed back from her temples. The torn green silk of her dress clung damply. The starved thinness of her gave her a strange beauty, clear and brittle, like sculptured ice.

She'd lived in alleys and cellars, hiding from the Hiltonists, because she wouldn't be Happy. She was strong, that girl. Like an unwanted cat that simply wouldn't die.

Avery sat in the pilot's chair, watching through the shaded port. He swung around as Falken got up. The exhaustion was gone from his square young face, but his eyes were still veiled and strange. Falken couldn't read them, but he sensed fear.

He asked, "How long have I slept?"

Avery shrugged. "The chronometer stopped. A long time, though. Twenty hours, perhaps."

Falken went to the controls. "Better go back now. We'll swing wide of Mercury, and perhaps we can get through." He hoped their constant velocity hadn't carried them too far for their fuel.

Relief surged over Avery's face. "The size of that Sun," he said jerkily. "It's terrifying. I never felt . . ."

He broke off sharply. Something about his tone brought Sheila's eyes wide open.

Suddenly, the bell of the mass-detector began to ring, a wild insistent jangle.

"Meteor!" cried Falken and leaped for the Visor screen. Then he froze, staring.

It was no meteor, rushing at them out of the vast blaze of the Sun. It was a planet.

A dark planet, black as the infinity behind it, barren and cruel as starvation, touched in its jagged peaks with subtle, phosphorescent fires.

Paul Avery whispered, "Good Lord! A planet, here? But it's impossible!"

Sheila Moore sprang up.

"No! Remember the old legends about Vulcan, the planet between Mercury and the Sun? Nobody believed in it, because they could never find it. But they could never explain Mercury's crazy orbit, either, except by the gravitational interference of another body."

Avery said, "Surely the Mercurian observatories would have found it?" A pulse began to beat in his strong white throat.

"It's there," snapped Falken impatiently. "And we'll crash it in a minute if we . . . Sheila! Sheila Moore!"

The dull glare from the ports caught the proud, bleak lines of his gypsy face, the sudden fire in his blue eyes.

"This is a world, Sheila! It might be a world for us, a world where Unregenerates could live, and wait!"

She gasped and stared at him, and Paul Avery said:

"Look at it, Falken! No one, nothing could live there."

Falken said softly, "Afraid to land and see?"

Yellow eyes burned into his, confused and wild. Then Avery turned jerkily away.

"No. But you can't land, Falken. Look at it."

Falken looked, using a powerful search-beam, probing. Vulcan was smaller even than Mercury. There was no atmosphere. Peaks like splinters of black glass bristled upward, revolving slowly in the Sun's tremendous blaze.

The beam went down into the bottomless dark of the canyons. There was nothing there, but the glassy rock and the dim glints of light through it.

"All the same," said Falken, "I'm going to land." If there was even a tiny chance, he couldn't let it slip.

Unregeneracy was almost dead in the inhabited worlds. Paul Avery was the only recruit in months. And it was dying in the miserable outer strongholds of independence.

Starvation, plague, cold, and darkness. Insecurity and danger, and the awful lost terror of humans torn from earth and light. Unless they could find a place of safety, with warmth and light and dirt to grow food in, where babies could be born and live, Gantry Hilton would soon have the whole Solar System for his toy.

There were no more protests. Falken set the ship down with infinite skill on a ledge on the night side. Then he turned, feeling the blood beat in his wrists and throat.

"Vac suits," he said. "There are two and a spare."

They got into them, shuffled through the airlock, and stood still, the first humans on an undiscovered world.

Lead weights in their boots held them so that they could walk. Falken thrust at the rock with a steel-shod alpenstock.

"It's like glass," he said. "Some unfamiliar compound, probably, fused out of raw force in the Solar disturbance that created the planets. That would explain its resistance to heat."

Radio headphones carried Avery's voice back to him clearly, and Falken realized that the stuff of the planet insulated against Solar waves, which would normally have blanketed communication.

"Whatever it is," said Avery, "it sucks up light. That's why it's never been seen. Only little glimmers seep through, too feeble for telescopes even on Mercury to pick up against the Sun. Its mass is too tiny for its transits to be visible, and it doesn't reflect."

"A sort of dark stranger, hiding in space," said Sheila, and shivered. "Look, Eric! Isn't that a cave mouth?"

Falken's heart gave a great leap of hope. There were caves on Pluto. Perhaps, in the hidden heart of this queer world. . . .

They went toward the opening. It was surprisingly warm. Falken guessed that the black rock diffused the Sun's heat instead of stopping it.

Thin ragged spires reared overhead, stabbing at the stars. Furtive glints of light came and went in ebon depths. The cave opened before them, and their torches showed glistening walls dropping sheer away into blackness.

Falken uncoiled a thousand-foot length of synthetic fiber rope from his belt. It was no larger than a spider web, and strong enough to hold Falken and Avery together. He tied one each of their metal boots to it and let it down.

It floated endlessly out, the lead weight dropping slowly in the light gravity. Eight hundred, nine hundred feet. When there were five feet of rope left in Falken's hand it stopped.

"Well," he said. "There is a bottom."

Paul Avery caught his arm. "You aren't going down?"

"Why not?" Falken scowled at him, puzzled. "Stay here, if you prefer. Sheila?"

"I'm coming with you."

"All right," whispered Avery. "I'll come.'" His amber eyes were momentarily those of a lion caught in a pit. Afraid, and dangerous.

Dangerous? Falken shook his head irritably He drove his alpenstock into a crack and made the rope fast.

"Hang onto it," he said. "We'll float like balloons, but be careful. I'll go first. If there's anything wrong down there, chuck off your other boot and climb up fast."

They went down, floating endlessly on the weighted rope. Little glints of light fled through the night-dark walls. It grew hot. Then Falken struck a jog in the cleft wall and felt himself sliding down a forty-five-degree offset. Abruptly, there was light.

Falken yelled, in sharp, wild warning.

The thing was almost on him. A colossus with burning eyes set on foot-long stalks, with fanged jaws agape and muscles straining.

Falken grabbed for his blaster. The quick motion over-balanced him. Sheila slid down on him and they fell slowly together, staring helplessly at destruction charging at them through a rainbow swirl of light.

The creature rushed by, in utter silence.

Paul Avery landed, his blaster ready. Falken and Sheila scrambled up, cold with the sweat of terror.

"What was it?" gasped Sheila.

Falken said shakily, "God knows!" He turned to look at their surroundings.

And swept the others back into the shadow of the cleft.

Riders hunted the colossus. Riders of a shape so mad that even in madness no human could have conceived them. Riders on steeds like the arrowing tails of comets, hallooing on behind a pack of nightmare hounds. . . .

Cold sweat drenched him. "How can they live without air?" he whispered. "And why didn't they see us?"

There was no answer. But they were safe, for the moment. The light, a shifting web of prismatic colors, showed nothing moving.

They stood on a floor of the glassy black rock. Above and on both sides walls curved away into the wild light—sunlight, apparently, splintered by the shell of the planet. Ahead there was an ebon plain, curving to match the curve of the vault.

Falken stared at it bitterly There was no haven here. No life as he knew it could survive in this pit. Yet there was life, of some mad sort. Another time, they might not escape.

"Better go back," he said wearily, and turned to catch the rope.

The cleft was gone.

Smooth and unbroken, the black wall mocked him. Yet he hadn't moved more than two paces. He smothered a swift stab of fear.

"Look for it," he snapped. "It must be here."

But it wasn't. They searched, and came again together, to stare at each other with eyes already a little mad.

Paul Avery laughed sharply. "There's something here," he said. "Something alive."

Falken snarled, "Of course, you fool! Those creatures. . . ."

"No. Something else. Something laughing at us."

"Shut up, Avery," said Sheila. "We can't go to pieces now."

"And we can't just stand here glaring." Falken looked out through the rainbow dazzle. "We may as well explore. Perhaps there's another way out."

Avery chuckled, without mirth. "And perhaps there isn't. Perhaps there was never a way in. What happened to it, Falken?"

"Control yourself," said Falken silkily, "or I'll rip off your oxygen valve. All right. Let's go."

They went a long way across the plain in the airless, unechoing silence, slipping on glassy rock, dazzled by the wheeling colors.

Then Falken saw the castle.

It loomed quite suddenly—a bulk of squat wings with queer, twisted turrets and straggling windows. Falken scowled. He was sure he hadn't seen it before. Perhaps the light . . .

They hesitated. Icy moth-wings flittered over Falken's skin. He would have gone around, but black walls seemed to stretch endlessly on either side of the castle.

"We go in," he said, and shuddered at the thought of meeting folk like those who hunted the flaming-eyed colossus.

Blasters ready, they went up flat titanic steps. A hall without doors stretched before them. They went down it.

Falken had a dizzy sense of change. The walls quivered as though with a wash of water over them. And then there were doors opening out of a round hall.

He opened one. There was a round hall beyond, with further doors. He turned back. The hall down which they had come had vanished. There were only doors. Hundreds of them, of odd shapes and sizes, like things imperfectly remembered.

Paul Avery began to laugh.

Falken struck him, hard, over the helmet. He stopped, and Sheila caught Falken's arm, pointing.

Shadows came, rushing and wheeling like monstrous birds. Cold dread caught Falken's heart. Shadows, hunting them . . .

He choked down the mad laughter rising in his own throat. He opened another door.

Halls, with doors. The shadows swept after them. Falken hurled the doors open, faster and faster, but there was never anything beyond but another hall, with doors.

His heart was gorged and painful. His clothing was cold on his sweating body. He plunged on and on through black halls and drifting shards of light, with the shadows dancing all around and doors, doors, doors.

Paul Avery made a little empty chuckle. "It's laughing," he mumbled and went down on the black floor. The shadows leaped.

Sheila's eyes were staring fire in her starved white face. Her terror shocked against Falken's brain and steadied it.

"Take his feet," he said harshly. "Take his feet."

They staggered on with their burden. And presently there were no more doors, and no roof overhead. Only the light and the glassy walls, and the dancing shadows.

The walls were thin in places. Through them Falken saw the dark colossus with its flaming eyes, straining through the spangled light. After it came the hounds and hunters, not gaining nor falling back, riding in blind absorption.

The walls faded, and the shadows. They were alone in the center of the black plain. Falken looked back at the castle.

There was nothing but the flat and naked rock.

He laid Avery down. He saw Sheila Moore fall beside him. He laughed, one small, mad chuckle. Then he crouched beside the others, his scarred gypsy face a mask of living stone.

Whether it was then, or hours later that he heard the voice, Falken never knew. But it spoke loudly in his mind, that voice. It brought him up, his futile blaster raised.

"You are humans," said the voice. "How wonderful!"

Falken looked upward, sensing a change in the light.

Something floated overhead. A ten-foot area of curdled glory, a core of blinding brilliance set in a lacy froth of fire.

The beauty of it caught Falken's throat. It shimmered with a sparkling opalescence, infinitely lovely—a living, tender flame floating in the rainbow light. It caught his heart, too, with a deep sadness that drifted in dim, faded colors beneath the brilliant veil.

It said, clearly as a spoken voice in his mind:

"Yes. I live, and I speak to you."

Sheila and Avery had risen. They stared, wide-eyed, and Sheila whispered, "What are you?"

The fire-thing coiled within itself. Little snapping flames licked from its edges, and its colors laughed.

"A female, isn't it? Splendid! I shall devise something very special." Colors rippled as its thoughts changed. "You amaze me, humans. I cannot read your minds, beyond thoughts telepathically directed at me, but I can sense their energy output.

"I had picked the yellow one for the strongest. He appeared to be so. Yet he failed, and you others fought through."

Avery stared at Falken with the dawn of an appalled realization in his amber eyes. Falken asked of the light:

"What are you?"

The floating fire dipped and swirled. Preening peacock tints rippled through it, to be drowned in fierce, proud scarlet. It said: "I am a child of the Sun."

It watched them gape in stunned amazement, and laughed with

mocking golden notes.

"I will tell you, humans. It will amuse me to have an audience not of my own creating. Watch!"

A slab of the glassy rock took form before them. Deep in it, a spot of brilliance grew:

It was a Sun, in the first blaze of its virile youth. It strode the path of its galactic orbit alone. Then, from the wheeling depths of space, a second Sun approached.

It was huge, burning with a blue-white radiance. There was a mating, and the nine worlds were born in a rush of supernal fire.

And there was life. Not on the nine burning planets. But in free space, little globes of fire, bits of the Sun itself shocked somehow to intelligence in the vast explosion of energy.

The picture blurred. The colors of the floating light were dulled and dreamy.

"There were many of us," it sighed. "We were like tiny Suns, living on the conversion of our own atoms. We played, in open space. . . ."

Dim pictures washed the screen, glories beyond human comprehension—a faded vision of splendor, of alien worlds and the great wheeling Suns of outer space. The voice murmured:

"Like Suns, we radiated our energy. We could draw strength from our parent, but not enough. We died. But I was stronger than the rest, and more intelligent. I built myself a shell."

"Built it!" whispered Avery. "But how?"

"All matter is built of raw energy, electron and proton existing in a free state. With a part of my own mass I built this world around myself, to hold the energy of the Sun and check the radiation of my own vitality.

"I have lived, where my race died. I have watched the planets cool and live and die. I am not immortal. My mass grows less as it drains away through my shell. But it will be a long, long time. I shall watch the Sun die, too."

The voice was silent. The colors were ashes of light. Falken was stricken with a great poignant grief.

Then, presently, the little malicious flames frothed to life again, and the voice said.

"My greatest problem is amusement. Here in this black shell I am forced to devise pleasures from my own imagination."

Falken gasped. "The hunters, the cleft that vanished, and that hellish castle?" He was suddenly cold and hot at once.

"Clever, eh? I created my hunt some eons ago. According to my plan the beast can neither escape nor the hunters catch him. But, owing to the uncertainty factor, there is one chance in some hundreds of billions that one or the other event may occur. It affords me endless amusement."

"And the castle?" said Falken silkily. "That amused you, too."

"Oh, yes! Your emotional reactions . . . most interesting!"

Falken raised his blaster and fired at the core of the light.

Living fire coiled and writhed. The Sun-child laughed.

"Raw energy only feeds me. What, are there no questions?"

Falken's voice was almost gentle. "Do you think of nothing but amusement?"

Savage colors rippled against the dim, sad mauves. "What else is there, to fill the time?"

Time. Time since little frozen Pluto was incandescent gas.

"You closed the opening we came through," said Avery abruptly.

"Of course."

"But you'll open it again? You'll let us go?"

The tone of his voice betrayed him. Falken knew, and Sheila.

"No," said Sheila throatily. "It won't let us go. It'll keep us up here to play with, until we die."

Ugly dark reds washed the Sun-child. "Death!" it whispered. "My creatures exist until I bid them vanish. But death, true death—that would be a supreme amusement!"

A desperate, helpless rage gripped Falken. The vast empty vault mocked him with his dead hopes. It jeered at him with solid walls that were built and shifted like smoke by the power of this lovely, soulless flame.

Built, and shifted . . .

Sudden fire struck his brain. He stood rigid, stricken dumb by the sheer magnificence of his idea. He began to tremble, and the wild hope swelled in him until his veins were gorged and aching.

He said, with infinite care, "You can't create real living creatures, can you?"

"No," said the Sun-child. "I can build the chemicals of their bodies, but the vital spark eludes me. My creatures are simply toys activated by the electrical interplay of atoms. They think, in limited ways, and they feel crude emotions, but they do not live in the true sense."

"But you can build other things? Rocks, soil, water, air?"

"Of course. It would take a great deal of my strength, and it would weaken my shell, since I should have to break down part of the rock to its primary particles and rebuild. But even that I could do, without serious loss."

There was silence. The blue distant fires flared in Falken's eyes. He saw the others staring at him. He saw the chances of failure bulk over him like black thunderheads, crowned with madness and death.

But his soul shivered in ecstasy at the thing that was in it.

The Sun-child said silkily, "Why should I do all this?"

"For amusement," whispered Falken. "The most colossal game you have ever had."

Brilliant colors flared. "Tell me, human!"

"I must make a bargain first."

"Why should I bargain? You're mine, to do with as I will."

"Quite. But we couldn't last very long. Why waste your imagination on the three of us when you might have thousands?"

Avery's amber eyes opened wide. A shocked incredulity slackened Sheila's rigid muscles. The voice cried:

"Thousands of humans to play with?"

The eager greed sickened Falken. Like a child wanting a bright toy—only the toys were human souls.

"Not until the bargain is made," he said.

"Well? What is the bargain? Quick!"

"Let us go, in return for the game which I shall tell you."

"I might lose you, and then have nothing."

"You can trust us," Falken insisted. He was shaking, and his nerves ached. "Listen. There are thousands of my people, living like hunted beasts in the deserts of the Solar System. They need a world, to survive at all. If you'll build them one in the heart of this planet, I'll bring them here.

"You wouldn't kill them. You'd let them live, to admire and praise you for saving them. It would amuse you just to watch them for some time. Then you could take one, once in a while, for a special game.

"I don't want to do this. But it's better that they should live that way than be destroyed."

"And better for you, too, eh?" The Sun-child swirled reflectively. "Breed men like cattle, always have a supply. It's a wonderful idea . . ."

"Then you'll do it?" Sweat dampened Falken's brow.

"Perhaps . . . Yes! Tell me, quickly, what you want!"

Falken swung to his stunned and unbelieving companions. He gripped an arm of each, painfully hard.

"Trust me. Trust me, for God's sake!" he whispered. Then, aloud, "Help me to tell it what we need."

There was a little laughing ripple of golden notes in the Sun-child's light, but Falken was watching Sheila's eyes. A flash of understanding crossed them, a glint of savage hope.

"Oxygen," she said. "Nitrogen, hydrogen, carbon dioxide . . ."

"And soil," said Falken. "Lime, iron, aluminum, silicon . . ."

They came to on a slope of raw, red earth, still wet from the rain. A range of low hills lifted in the distance against a strange black sky. Small tattered clouds drifted close above in the rainbow's light.

Falken got to his feet. As far as he could see there were rolling stretches of naked earth, flecked with brassy pools and little ruddy streams. He opened his helmet and breathed the warm wet air. He let the rich soil trickle through his fingers and thought of the Unregenerates in their frozen burrows.

He smiled, because there were tears in his hard blue eyes.

Sheila gave a little sobbing laugh and cried, "Eric, it's done!"

Paul Avery lifted dark golden eyes to the hills and was silent.

There was a laughing tremble of color in the air where the Sun-child floated. Small wicked flames drowned the sad, soft mauves. The Sun-child said:

"Look, Eric Falken. There, behind you."

Falken turned—and looked into his own face.

It stood there, his own lean body in the worn vac suit, his own gypsy face and the tangle of frosted curls. Only the eyes were different. The chill, distant blue was right, but there were spiteful flecks of gold, a malicious sparkle that was like . . . .

"Yes," purred the Sun-child. "Myself, a tiny particle, to activate the shell. A perfect likeness, no?"

A slow, creeping chill touched Falken's heart. "Why?" he asked.

"Long ago I learned the art of lying from men. I lied about reading minds. Your plan to trick me into building this world and then destroy me was plain on the instant of conception."

Laughing wicked colors coiled and spun.

"Oh, but I'm enjoying this! Not since I built my shell have I had such a game! Can you guess why I made your double?"

Falken's lips were tight with pain, his eyes savage with remorse at his own stupidity.

"It—he will go in my ship to bring my people here."

He knew that the Sun-child had picked his unwitting brain as cleanly as any Hiltonist psycho-search.

In sudden desperation he drew his blaster and shot at the mocking likeness. Before he tripped the trigger-stud a wall of ebon glass was raised between them. The blast-ray slid away in harmless fire and died, burned out.

The other Falken turned and strode away across the new land. Falken watched him out of sight, not moving nor speaking, because there was nothing to do, nothing to say.

The lovely wicked fire of the Sun-child faded suddenly.

"I am tired," it said. "I shall suckle the Sun, and rest."

It floated away. For all his agony, Falken felt the heart-stab of its sad, dim colors. It faded like a wisp of lonely smoke into the splintered light.

Presently there was a blinding flash and a sharp surge of air as a fissure was opened. Falken saw the creature, far away, pressed to the roof of the vault and pulsing as it drank the raw blaze of the Sun.

"Oh, God," whispered Falken. "Oh, God, what have I done?"

Falken laughed, one harsh wild cry. Then he stood quite still his hands at his sides, his face a mask cut deep in dark stone.

"Eric," whispered Sheila. "Please. I can't be brave for you all the time."

He was ashamed of himself then. He shook the black despair away with cynical fatalism.

"All right, Sheila. We'll be heroes to the bitter end. You, Avery. Get your great brain working. How can we save our people, and, incidentally, our own skins?"

Avery flinched as though some swift fear had stabbed him. "Don't ask me, Falken. Don't!"

"Why not? What the devil's the matter . . . ." Falken broke off sharply. Something cold and fierce and terrifying came into his face. "Just a minute, Avery," he said gently. "Does that mean you think you know a way?"

"I . . . For God's sake, let me alone!"

"You do know a way," said Falken inexorably. "Why shouldn't I ask you, Paul Avery? Why shouldn't you try to save your people?"

Golden eyes met his, desperate, defiant, bewildered, and pitiful all at once.

"They're not my people," whispered Avery.

They were caught, then, in a strange silence. Soundless wheeling rainbows brushed the new earth, glimmered in the brassy pools. Far up on the black crystal of the vault the Sun-child pulsed and breathed. And there was stillness, like the morning of creation.

Eric Falken took one slow, taut step, and said, "Who are you?"

The answer whispered across the raw red earth.

"Miner Hilton, the son of Gantry."

* * * *

Falken raised the blaster, forgotten in his hand. Miner Hilton, who had been Paul Avery, looked at it and then at Falken's face, a shield of dark iron over cold, terrible flame.

He shivered, but he didn't move, nor speak.

"You know a way to fight that thing," said Falken, very softly, in his throat. "I want to kill you. But you know a way."

"I—I don't know. I can't . . ." Golden tortured eyes went to Sheila Moore and stayed there, with a dreadful lost intensity.

Falken's white teeth showed. "You want to tell, Miner Hilton. You want to help us, don't you? Because of Sheila!"

Young Hilton's face flamed red, and then went white. Sheila cried sharply, "Eric, don't! Can't you see he's suffering?"

But Falken remembered Kitty, and the babies who were born and died on freezing rock, without sun or shelter. He said, "She'd never have you, Hilton. And I'll tell you this. Perhaps I can't force out of you what you know. But if I can't, I swear to God I'll kill you with my own hands."

He threw back his head and laughed suddenly "Gantry Hilton's son—in love with an Unregenerate!"

"Wait, Eric." Sheila Moore put a hand on his arm to stop him, and went forward. She took Miner Hilton by the shoulders and looked up at him, and said, "It isn't so impossible, Miner Hilton. Not if what I think is true."

Falken stared at her in stunned amazement, beyond speech or movement. Then his heart was torn with sudden pain, and he knew, with the clarity of utter truth, that he loved Sheila Moore.

She said to Miner Hilton, "Why did you do this? And how?"

Young Hilton's voice was flat and strained. He made a move as though to take her hands from his shoulders, but he didn't. He stared across her red-gold head, at Falken.

"Something had to be done to stamp out the Unregenerates. They're a barrier to complete peace, a constant trouble. Eric Falken is their god, as—as Sheila said. If we could trap him, the rest would be easy. We could cure his people.

"My father couldn't do it himself. He's old, and too well-known.

"He sent me, because mine is the only other brain that could stand what I had to do. My father has trained me well.

"To get me by the psycho-search, my father gave me a temporary brain pattern. After I was accepted as a refugee, I established mental contact with him. . . ."

"Mental contact," breathed Falken. "That was it. That's why you were always so tired, why I couldn't shake pursuit."

"Go on," said Sheila, with a queer gentleness.

Hilton stared into space, without seeing.

"I almost had you in Losangles, Falken, but you were too quick for the Guards. Then, when we were trapped at Mercury, I tried to make you sleep. I was leading those ships, too.

"But I was tired, and you fought too well, you and Sheila. After that we were too close to the Sun. My thought waves wouldn't carry back to the ships."

He looked at Falken, and then down at Sheila's thin face.

"I didn't know there were people like you," he whispered. "I didn't know men could feel things, and fight for them like that. In my world, no one wants anything, no one fights, or tries . . . And I have no strength. I'm afraid."

Sheila's green eyes caught his, compelled them.

"Leave that world," she said. "You see it's wrong. Help us to make it right again."

In that second, Falken saw what she was doing. He was filled with admiration, and joy that she didn't really care for Hilton— and then doubt, that perhaps she did.

Miner Hilton closed his eyes. He struck her hands suddenly away and stepped back, and his blaster came ready into his hand.

"I can't," he whispered. His lips were white. "My father has taught me. He trusts me. And I believe in him. I must!"

Hilton looked where the glow of the Sun-child pulsed against ebon rock. "The Unregenerates won't trouble us anymore."

He raised the muzzle of his blaster to his head.

It was then that Falken remembered his was empty. He dropped it and sprang. He shocked hard against Hilton's middle, struck him down, clawing for his gun arm. But Hilton was heavy, and strong.

He rolled away and brought his barrel lashing down across Falken's temple. Falken crouched, dazed and bleeding, in the mud.

He laughed, and said, "Why don't you kill me, Hilton?"

Hilton looked from Falken's uncowed, snarling face to Sheila. The blaster slipped suddenly from his fingers. He covered his face with his hands and was silent, shivering.

Falken said, with curious gentleness, "That proves it. You've got to have faith in a thing, to kill or die for it."

Hilton whispered, "Sheila!" She smiled and kissed him, and Falken looked steadfastly away, wiping the blood out of his eyes.

Hilton grasped suddenly at the helmet of his vac-suit. He talked, rapidly, as he worked.

"The Sun-child creates with the force of its mind. It understands telekinesis, the control of the basic electrical force of the universe by thought, just as the wise men of our earth understood it. The men who walked on the water, and moved mountains, and healed the sick.

"We can only attack it through its mind. We'll try to weaken its thought-force, destroy anything it sends against us."

His fingers flashed between the helmet radio and the repair kit which is a part of every vac suit, using wires, spare parts, tools.

"There," said Hilton, after a long time. "Now yours."

Falken gave him his helmet. "Won't the Sun-child know what we're doing?" he asked, rather harshly.

Hilton shook his fair head. "It's weak now. It won't think about us until it has fed. Perhaps two hours more."

"Can you read its thoughts?" demanded Falken sourly.

"A very little," said Hilton, and Sheila laughed, quietly.

Hilton worked feverishly. Falken watched his deft fingers weaving a bewildering web of wires between the three helmets, watched him shift and change, tune and adjust. He watched the Sun-child throb and sparkle as the strength of the Sun sank into it. He watched Sheila Moore, staring at Hilton with eyes of brilliant green.

He never knew how much time passed. Only that the Sun-child gave a little rippling sigh of light and floated down. The fissure closed above it. Sheila caught her breath, sharp between her teeth.

Hilton rose. He said rapidly,

"I've done the best I can. It's crude, but the batteries are strong. The helmets will pick up and amplify the energy-impulses of our brains. We'll broadcast a single negative impulse, opposed to every desire the Sun-thing has.

"Stay close together, because if the wires are broken between the helmets we lose power, and it's going to take all the strength we have to beat that creature."

Falken put on his helmet. Little copper discs, cut from the sheet in the repair kit and soldered to wires with Hilton's blaster, fitted to his temples. Through the vision ports he could see the web of wires that ran from the three helmets through a maze of spare grids and a condenser, and then into the slender shaft of a crude directional antenna.

Hilton said, "Concentrate on the single negative, No."

Falken looked at the lovely shimmering cloud, coming toward them.

"It won't be easy," he said grimly, "to concentrate."

Sheila's eyes were savage and feral, watching that foam of living flame. Hilton's face was hidden. He said, "Switch on your radios."

Power hummed from the batteries. Falken felt a queer tingle in his brain.

The Sun-child hovered over them. Its mind-voice was silent, and Falken knew that the electrical current in his helmet was blanking his own thoughts.

They linked arms. Falken set his brain to beating out an impulse, like a radio signal, opposing the negative of his mind to the positive of the Sun-child's.

Falken stood with the others on spongy, yielding soil. Dim plant-shapes rose on all sides as far as he could see, forming an impenetrable tangle of queer geometric shapes that made him reel with a sense of spatial distortion.

Overhead, in a sea-green sky, three tiny suns wheeled in mad orbits about a common center. There was a smell in the air, a rotting stench that was neither animal or vegetable.

Falken stood still, pouring all his strength into that single mental command to stop.

The tangled geometric trees wavered momentarily. Dizzily, through the wheeling triple suns, the Sun-child showed, stabbed through with puzzled, angry scarlet.

The landscape steadied again. And the ground began to move.

It crawled in small hungry wavelets about Falken's feet. The musky, rotten smell was heavy as oil. Sheila and Hilton seemed distant and unreal, their faces hidden in the helmets.

Falken gripped them together and drove his brain to its task. He knew what this was. The reproduction of another world, remembered from the Sun-child's youth. If they could only stand still, and not think about it. . . .

He felt the earth lurch upward, and guessed that the Sun-child had raised its creation off the floor of the cavern.

The earth began to coil away from under his feet.

For a giddy instant Falken saw the true world far below, and the Sun-child floating in rainbow light.

It was angry. He could tell that from its color. Then suddenly the anger was drowned in a swirl of golden motes.

It was laughing. The Sun-child was laughing.

Falken fought down a sharp despair. A terrible fear of falling oppressed him. He heard Sheila scream. The world closed in again.

Sheila Moore looked at him from between two writhing trees.

He hadn't let her go. But she was there. Hairy branches coiled around her, tore her vac-suit. She shrieked. . . .

Falken cried out and went forward. Something held him. He fought it off, driven by the agony in Sheila's cry.

Something snapped thinly. There was a flaring shock inside his helmet. He fell, and staggered up and on, and the hungry branches whipped away from the girl.

She stood there, her thin white body showing through the torn vac-suit, and laughed at him.

He saw Miner Hilton crawling dazed on the living ground, to-ward the thing that looked like Sheila and laughed with mocking golden motes in its eyes.

A vast darkness settled on Falken's soul. He turned. Sheila Moore crouched where he had thrown her from him, in his strug-gle to help the lying shell among the trees.

He went and picked her up. He said to Miner Hilton, "Can we fix these broken wires?"

Hilton shook his head. The shock of the breaking seemed to have steadied him a little. "No," he said. "Too much burned out."

"Then we're beaten." Falken turned a bitter, snarling face to the green sky, raised one futile fist and shook it. Then he was si-lent, looking at the others.

Sheila Moore said softly, "This is the end, isn't it?"

Falken nodded. And Miner Hilton said, "I'm not afraid now." He looked at the trees that hung over them, waiting, and shook his head. "I don't understand. Now that I know I'm going to die, I'm not afraid."

Sheila's green eyes were soft and misty. She kissed Hilton, slowly and tenderly, on the lips.

Falken turned his back and stared at the twisted ugly trees. He didn't see them. And he wasn't thinking of the Unregenerates and the world he'd won and then lost.

Sheila's hand touched him. She whispered, "Eric . . ."

Her eyes were deep, glorious green. Her pale starved face had the brittle beauty of wind-carved snow. She held up her arms and smiled.

Falken took her and buried his gypsy face in the raw gold of her hair.

"How did you know?" he whispered. "How did you know I loved you?"

"I just—knew."

"And Hilton?"

"He doesn't love me, Eric. He loves what I stand for. And anyway . . . I can say this now, because we're going to die. I've loved you since I first saw you. I love you more than Tom, and I'd have died for him."

Hungry tree branches reached for them, barely too short. Buds were shooting up underfoot. But Falken forgot them, the alien life and the wheeling suns that were only a monstrous dream, and the Sun-child who dreamed them.

For that single instant he was happy, as he had not been since Kitty was lost.

Presently he turned and smiled at Hilton, and the wolf look was gone from his face. Hilton said quietly, "Maybe she's right, about me. I don't know. There's so much I don't know. I'm sorry I'm not going to live to find out."

"We're all sorry," said Falken, "about not living." A sudden sharp flare lighted his eyes. "Wait a minute!" he whispered. "There may be a chance. . . ."

He was taut and quivering with terrible urgency, and the buds grew and yearned upward around their feet.

"You said we could only attack it through its mind. But there may be another way. Its memories, its pride. . . ."

He raised his scarred gypsy face to the green sky and shouted, "You, Child of the Sun! Listen to me! You have beaten us. Go ahead and kill us. But remember this. You're a child of the Sun, and we're only puny humans, little ground-crawlers, shackled with weakness and fear.

"But we're greater than you! Always and forever, greater than you!"

The writhing trees paused, the buds faltered in their hungry growth. Faintly, very faintly, the landscape flickered. Falken's voice rose to a ringing shout.

"You were a child of the Sun. You had the galaxy for a toy, all the vast depths of space to play in. And what did you do? You sealed yourself like a craven into a black tomb, and lost all your greatness in the whimsies of a wicked child.

"You were afraid of your destiny. You were too weak for your own strength. We fought you, we little humans, and our strength was so great that you had to beat us by a lying trick.

"You can read our minds, Sun-child. Read them. See whether we fear you. And see whether we respect you, you who boast of your parentage and dream dreams of lost glory, and hide in a dark hole like a frightened rat!"

For one terrible moment the alien world was suffused with a glare of scarlet—anger so great that it was almost tangible. Then it greyed and faded, and Falken could see Sheila's face, calm and smiling, and Hilton's fingers locked in hers.

The ground dropped suddenly. Blurred trees writhed against a fading sky, and the suns went out in ebon shadow. Falken felt clean earth under him. The rotting stench was gone.

He looked up. The Sun-child floated overhead, under the rocky vault. They were back in the cavern world.

The Sun-child's voice spoke in his brain, and its fires were a smoldering, dusky crimson.

"What was that you said, human?"

"Look into my mind and read it. You've thrown away your greatness. We had little, compared to you, but we kept it. You've won, but your very winning is a shame to you, that a child of the Sun should stoop to fight with little men."

The smoldering crimson burned and grew, into glorious wicked fire that was sheer fury made visible. Falken felt death coiling to strike him out of that fire. But he faced it with bitter, mocking eyes, and he was surprised, even then, that he wasn't afraid.

And the raging crimson fire faded and greyed, was quenched to a trembling mist of sad, dim mauves.

"You are right," whispered the Sun-child. "And I am shamed."

The ashes of burned-out flame stirred briefly. "I think I began to realize that when you fought me so well. You, Falken, who let your love betray you, and then shook your fist at me. I could kill you, but I couldn't break you. You made me remember . . ."

Deep in the core of the Sun-child there was a flash of the old proud scarlet.

"I am a child of the Sun, with the galaxy to play with. I have so nearly forgotten. I have tried to forget, because I knew that what

I did was weak and shameful and craven. But you haven't let me forget, Falken. You've forced me to see, and know.

"You have made me remember. Remember! I am very old. I shall die soon, in open space. But I wish to see the Sun unveiled, and play again among the stars. The hunger has torn me for eons, but I was afraid. Afraid of death!

"Take this world, in payment for the pain I caused you. My creature will return here in Falken's ship and vanish on the instant of landing. And now . . ."

The scarlet fire burned and writhed. Shafts of joyous gold pierced through it. The Sun-child trembled, and its little foaming flames were sheer glory, the hearts of Sun-born opals.

It rose in the rainbow air, higher and higher, rushing in a cloud of living light toward the black crystal of the vault.

Once more there was a blinding flash and a quick sharp rush of air. Faintly, in Falken's mind, a voice said, "Thank you, human! Thank you for waking me from a dying sleep!"

A last wild shout of color on the air. And then it was gone, into open space and the naked fire of the Sun, and the rocky roof was whole.

Three silent people stood on the raw red earth of a new world.